Six feet apart

LOVE IN QUARANTINE

This is a work of fiction. Names, characters, places, and incidents are products of the author's imagination or are used fictitiously and are not to be construed as real. Any resemblance to actual events, locales, organizations, or persons, living or dead, is entirely coincidental.

FIRST EDITION

ISBN 978-1-7354950-2-6

LOVE IN QUARANTINE

ELENA GREYROCK

For Arturo Augustus

for his encouragement, faith, and our collaboration in making this book a reality!

Author's Note:

Thank you so much for reading **Six Feet Apart: Love in Quarantine**. If you enjoyed it, please consider leaving a review or recommending it to a friend. I personally read every review as I gain insight from you, the reader, on my storylines and character development.

This is the first book in The Luna James Trilogy. If you enjoyed it please consider reading the second book in the trilogy, **Stryker Strikes Back**, a romantic suspense filled thriller set in a Post-Pandemic world.

If you are interested in seeing full lyrics to the original songs the main character plays, they are in the back pages of the book.

Want to follow me on social media and see my writing progress, photos from my daily life, and interesting new places I visit for inspiration and fun.

Follow me here: *Facebook - Twitter - Instagram*

Thank you again for your support!
Elena Greyrock

CHAPTER 1

FREEDOM IN AMERICA has vanished. The year is 2025. Luna James is alone, contained in her small New York City apartment. She's half listening to the world news broadcast blaring on the television.

"It has been five years since COVID-19. Cities are at the center of the Pandemic and mostly deserted. And for most of us our worlds have shrunk to the size of our homes." The female newscaster's voice is somber.

"Thousands of people now refuse to leave their homes and have developed FOGO, or the fear of going out… Dr. Schaeffer, you are an expert on infectious disease and part of the federal response team to minimize the effect of the virus over the last five years…please explain to our viewers how we got here…"

"Certainly." A man's head and shoulders appear on screen. His face is pale and worn. His hair is short and completely white, and he keeps pushing up his glasses that are slowly sliding down his nose.

"Let me explain the evolution of our response as a country. The United States was unprepared and in denial the virus would arrive with such vengeance. We took little precaution. Due to the lack of leadership from the federal government it took us two years for the response to COVID to level off. When the vaccine did arrive, things were better for a short time. That was until the virus kept mutating every six months. So, keeping up with the virus became difficult and unmanageable and the death rate again soared. Now that we have a better handle on testing with the Rapid DNA technology and the centralized database tracking the movements of all Americans, we are in a much better place to deal with COVID-25."

"So Dr. Schaeffer, are you saying the Pandemic will never go away?" the female newscaster asks fearfully. "How will we live? What should we expect?"

Luna points the remote at the woman's face and clicks off the television. It's a warm June evening and she misses going to the gym every day. She pulls on her lilac leggings and struggles into the matching sports bra top. The pastel purple color compliments her brown skin. She picks up her house keys, stopping for a moment to admire herself in the full-length mirror. She knows her body is flawless, her stomach impossibly flat, her cleavage peeking out of her top. Luna lets out a deep sigh, grabs her boombox, slips on her face mask, and pushes open her apartment door.

The roof is on the fourteenth floor, and halfway up the staircase Luna stops for a breath. Once she recovers and is breathing normally, she switches hands and lugs the heavy radio the rest of the way up the steps. Her small Bluetooth speakers had fizzled out, and she could not find them in stock anywhere online. Another symptom of the

Pandemic. She put the enormous radio on the ledge. It's a Bumpboxx Ultra Bluetooth boombox—a gift from her best friend, Santana, one Christmas prior to the Pandemic, when going retro was back in style. Luna loved the stereo's colorful graffiti design—it was so 90s.

Stryker is scrolling through his phone looking at the *Flikrz* posts of the hot girls he used to date. He sees meticulously staged photos of the women in sexy club outfits, or tiny bikinis on the beach, or lounging by the pool drinking margaritas with their girlfriends. Each post includes the hashtag #BTV2020, aka "Before the Virus 2020."

Frustrated, Stryker lets out a groan and tosses his phone onto the other end of the couch. He misses his one-night hookups with numerous women. He can't be bothered with dating apps that offer mutual masturbation. Certainly he can save those app fees and do that alone watching porn online.

Life now is all about "exclusive relationships." If you want any possibility of getting laid, each person has to prove they are virus free and obtain certification papers from the United States federal government. But the virus keeps mutating, making certification papers valid for only two weeks if that.

Bitter, he sits there for a moment, thinking of all the girls his couch endured—Rebecca, Brittany, Michelle, and so many more. He remembers Michelle in particular. She'd made so much noise when he was satisfying her every need that his irate neighbor banged loudly on his wall. Stryker smiles at that memory, then begins rubbing his temples in a circular motion. He thinks, What am I even doing? Those days are gone forever.

Relationships are not Stryker's thing. He stands up and runs his fingers through his platinum blond hair, catching his reflection in the window, proud he has finally perfected how to dye his hair at home. He knows the color accentuates his magnetic blue eyes. When he was working out in the gym, he always caught lustful glances from numerous women—and loved it!

With his acoustic guitar in hand, he steps out onto the fire escape and plays a melancholy song while looking at the sun setting between the buildings. Then he sees her, on the rooftop of the building across from his. A young Black woman is gyrating her sensuous body to Spanish music blaring from an old-school boombox. Her curvaceous body gives the impression of a dancing silhouette against the pink sky.

Luna takes off her face mask and turns the knob on the stereo. She quickly finds the signal on her iPhone and begins dancing the samba furiously to the Spanish beat. It's part of her latest Zumba routine she has spent endless hours learning in her cramped apartment. After only a few songs it happens. Luna is so caught up in the music she gets dangerously close to the side of the building, dancing wildly with her eyes closed. She turns and bumps the radio with her hip and in an instant, she watches it tumble off the roof into the alleyway below. Horrified, she lets out a shrill scream and then puts her hands over her mouth. Has she killed someone below? She's terrified to look. Will she see a bloody body sprawled on the sidewalk beneath her? Slowly she looks down and sees him for the first time, a tall muscular man on a fire escape in the building across from her. He's standing up holding a guitar.

"Nice try, you just missed me. Do you want to try it again? I think it might be salvageable," Stryker says with a glimpse of sarcasm.

He's leaning on the fire escape's metal railing, staring up at her. Luna's mouth is open, one because of the stereo tumbling off the roof and two she thinks, Damn, this guy is so hot! He looks like a cross between Zac Efron and Paul Walker. Living in New York City, Luna saw random handsome men all the time, on the subway, walking down the street, waiters in restaurants, and these men simply had no effect on her. She could care less. *But this man, this man's looks are remarkable.* She begins to quiver, her heart beating rapidly. She shuts her mouth and swallows hard, trying to gather herself and appear nonchalant. She has no words.

"What's your name?" Stryker asks.

He can see the effect his looks have on her. This is nothing new, he's used to it and lavishes in the attention.

"Luna," she says quietly.

"What?" Stryker inquires, holding his hand up to his ear.

O-M-G! Luna thinks, catching her breath. She can barely stand it she's so attracted to him. "Luna!" she replies this time in a loud voice, almost shouting. She stresses the Lu in her name, saying LuuuNa.

"Ah, Luna…I'm Stryker," Stryker says.

"Whaaat?" Stryker sounds like a made-up name and she thinks, Oh here we go.

"My name is Stryker. Stryker Caine," Stryker says proudly.

Luna rolls her eyes. "That sounds like a name out of *Star Wars*, that's not really your name," she says in disbelief.

"Oh, but it is." It's true, it's my God given name. My parents are very theatrical!" Stryker explains, spreading his arms out for emphasis.

He saw her eyes scanning his body as he said this. Good, he thinks, she's all mine. Stryker is amazed by her beauty. *She is stunning…and so natural looking.* Luna nervously twirls a strand of her long straight black hair around her finger. Her lustrous hair is past her shoulders, resting on her breasts. She has large expressive doe eyes and full lips. Stryker and Luna look at each other for a moment, not saying anything. It's clear there's an intense mutual attraction.

"Anyway, you don't need that ridiculous boombox. I can play better music for you to dance to," Stryker says, strumming his guitar.

He begins playing a Spanish sounding tune. He sings:

Feeling so alive on a sun-drenched day
Wind swept hair all around her face
Her laughter seems to come from every side
Fills up the air and takes me for a ride
Time was never better with the top pulled down
We make our way through gas filled towns
Full throttle speed another pitstop
Wheels spinning up to a coffee shop

Stryker watches Luna lean on the ledge, stretching her body to hear him play. He continues singing.

Fading from ourselves and chasing down the sun

No better time to be on the run

Time was never better with the top pulled down

We make our way through gas filled towns

Oh my God and he sings! Luna realizes he's beyond handsome and talented. As Stryker finishes singing the second verse, her shyness suddenly emerges and a feeling of sensory overload rushes over her. *I have to get out of here!*

"Very nice," she says, clapping halfheartedly, but I have to go now."

Stryker stops playing and stares up at her. What? he thinks. Where the hell does she need to go, we are all in quarantine.

"Ok," he says, pretending to be disinterested. "Maybe we will see each other again."

He has the last word and gingerly climbs through the window back into his apartment.

It's been almost ten days since Luna has danced on her building's rooftop. Ever since Stryker Caine serenaded her there, she avoids going up altogether. And Luna is mad.

"Why should I let some man control my thoughts and what I enjoy!" she says to herself, peering at her beautiful reflection in the bathroom mirror.

She opens the medicine cabinet, takes out the toothpaste, and spreads the minty gel on her toothbrush. Scowling at herself in the mirror, she brushes aggressively.

Damn him! Why is he taking up space in my brain? Probably because he is so God damn good looking!

Luna spits out the toothpaste into the sink with disgust

and runs the water. It's 8:56 a.m. and she has a 9:00 a.m. 123VideoMe meeting with her colleagues from the online magazine *Fashiondemic*. She rushes dressing into a light pink button-down shirt and yoga leggings. Luna loves she now works from home five days a week due to the Pandemic. She doesn't miss anyone from the office, not the water cooler conversations she would painfully have to listen to and pretend to be interested in. Not the lunches she would get invited to that she would always awkwardly decline. Luna is free from all that socializing and is truly on board with the mandated social distancing credo.

"Good morning!" Luna says happily, waving at the tiny camera lens in her laptop cover.

Two people are already on the screen—Luna's boss, Meghan Kennedy, a woman in her fifties with harsh wrinkles on her face is on the left. Alex Mitchell, a young energetic writer, is on the right. Darcy Brooks, a fashion editor with enormous teeth and an overbite, suddenly pops onto the middle of the computer screen.

"Good morning," Darcy says in a sing-song voice.

Darcy always dresses exquisitely in either Chanel or some other French designer. Today she's wearing a navy silk chiffon blouse with ruffles, her dried out mousy blonde hair is in a perfect messy bun on the top of her head.

"All right." Meghan Kennedy begins talking immediately, not indulging in any pleasantries. "Team, we are moving quickly in a different direction, and I need you all to step it up!"

Everyone on the call sits up in their chairs, not knowing what's coming next.

"*Fashiondemic*," Meghan continues, "is being acquired by Utmost Maximum by the end of the third quarter, and *Fashiondemic* is expected to have doubled its revenue by that time!

"What this means for you three specifically is..." Meghan pauses, her eyes open wide, her speech animated, "*Alex,* I expect *you* to bring me the very best article ideas, not ho-hum articles, bring me something with some meat on it!"

Alex nods his head up and down.

"Got it!" he says unequivocally.

"*Darcy,* bring me fashion that no one has ever seen before," Meghan says in a commanding voice.

"—and *Luna*, make both *Fashiondemic* and Utmost Maximum visible everywhere on Social!

"Got it?" Meghan has finished talking.

"Yes, got it, got it!" Luna and Darcy say almost in unison.

"Good," Meghan says dryly, and with a click, she disappears off the computer screen.

Alex, Darcy, and Luna are left on the 123VideoMe call. Each of them is afraid to say a word in case Meghan pops back onto the meeting.

"Okay, talk to you all later," Alex says, breaking the silence, and he is gone from view.

"Bye, girl," Darcy says with attitude, waving, and poof she's gone as well.

Luna slowly closes the lid of her computer, dazed, blinking her eyes hard.

Stryker taps the keys of his iPhone, searching Luna's name on Google. Even though he does not know her last name, he does know where she lives, and Luna is an uncommon name. After fifteen minutes he finds her last name.

"Bingo!" Stryker says aloud. "Miss Luna James, I've got you now."

He searches in image results next and finds a cheerful headshot of her on *WorkDawgs.com*. Her business profile reveals Luna works at *Fashiondemic*. Her black hair was curly in the photo and she was smiling. Next Stryker looks up her social profiles and surprisingly her *Flikrz* profile is locked, as is her Facebook profile.

That's weird. She's a social media manager and her accounts are private? That does not add up.

He gazes at her *WorkDawgs.com* photo—he cannot get her out of his mind. Luna is so beautiful. He has never been so attracted to any woman before and knows he can't just simply message her through the WorkDawgs website. He would come off as the stalker he is. *What am I going to do now? How am I ever going to see the elusive Luna James again?* He is hungry, irritable, and realizes he has nothing to eat in his apartment.

"I guess it's time to put the gloves on," Stryker says in annoyance.

He hates going to the grocery store in the Pandemic world. What was previously a mundane task has turned into a nerve-wracking ordeal. Is the virus lurking on food packaging and on produce? Anguished grocery shopping has become the sad ritual of every New Yorker, but nonetheless, Stryker has not gotten used to it. He is not on board.

৵

Luna is strategic about her grocery shopping, choosing to do it at off-peak hours. She goes to Pure Foods because she feels it's a "cleaner" supermarket. Most of the products and produce at Pure Foods are organic and more expensive. While she waits in line outside the entrance, she looks at the people ahead of her. Everyone is emptily gazing at their phones except for a tall thin Black woman dressed in a full body white hazmat suit with plastic booties over her shoes. Luna sighs through her mask. She knows most people have just accepted the sad situation in this Pandemic world while others still take the world's state of panic to the extreme and take every precaution to protect themselves. Once she is outside the supermarket door, Luna presents the clerk with documents detailing her health status, which the clerk checks and photographs. He then scans her forehead for temperature before allowing her inside. Luna follows the blue directional arrows on the floor and makes her way cautiously through the supermarket aisles. She's carrying a small shopping basket and walks up and down the inner aisles where the non-perishables are shelved, studying the products before daring to pick one up.

Stryker is already in the supermarket, maneuvering his shopping cart around the outer aisles. He doesn't have a strategy for shopping in a Pandemic, but he's hoping to score some meat. His t-shirt reads, "Meet Me After the Pandemic." He knows he looks good, his body is perfectly symmetrical, his chest is wide and taut, his legs in his loose-fitting board shorts have just the right amount of muscle. Then he spots her, toward the end of one of the aisles. It's Luna. She's wearing tight black yoga pants and a conservative pink button-up shirt. Stryker's first instinct is to call out her name "Luna" and wave at her like he's a long-lost cousin. Instead he pushes his shopping carriage the wrong way up the aisle.

Luna hears a cart approaching, the rickety steel wheels clanking together. Then the sound stops and she hears a man's voice.

"Why don't you dance on the roof anymore? I have been missing you," Stryker says confidently through his mask. He respects her space, standing six feet away.

Oh my God, it's him! Luna thinks as her cheeks flush. *Play it cool, play it cool. He can't see my face beneath my mask.* Luna pauses then says, "Because I'm just a poor working girl and my radio is broken…not that it's any of your business."

She is glaring at him. *Look at him looking so delicious, wearing that obnoxious t-shirt. He knows full well as the rest of the planet does the Pandemic will never be over.*

Dang, Stryker says to himself, boy is she giving me an attitude. He is not used to it. Most women would be stammering at his attention. Maybe she needs to get laid as much as he does.

"I can lend you my radio," Stryker says with a smile in his eyes, almost winking at her.

They stand for a moment face to face, no words spoken. Luna feels herself giving in. *Oh, what the hell, it might be fun.*

CHAPTER 2

LIVING THE PANDEMIC life has been a hard adjustment for Santana. He's a full-time Zumba instructor and Luna's best friend. He'd thrived on being the center of attention, teaching his packed Zumba classes throughout Manhattan. Now he teaches classes for only four people at a time, and the mood and his energy are just not the same. Santana is riding in a *UFetchr*, heading to Luna's house. She said she had something important to tell him, so he's making the long trek from his place in Queens to Washington Heights where Luna lives.

"Knockety knock," Santana says aloud while giving two vigorous knocks on her apartment door.

Luna opens the door, rushing him inside. "Come in, come in," she says breathlessly.

Santana's hazel eyes look inquisitively at Luna as he steps over the threshold. He is wearing his usual attire of a black muscle top, black shorts, and black sneakers. Santana looks around Luna's living room and sees items of clothing strewn everywhere on top of the living room furniture.

"Have you been robbed?" Santana asks, looking at the mess in the room.

"I met a guy," Luna says proudly. "And he's hot!"

Santana is surprised. Even in a pre-Pandemic world, Luna ignored all the handsome New York City men Santana lusted for.

"Ree-a-lly,' Santana says. "Spill it!"

Luna is more than happy to.

"He's blond, has blue eyes, an amazing body. An incredible face—oh my God, he is so hot!" Luna says joyously. "I'm going to his apartment later today, and I have no idea what to wear. Help me Santana. Pleeese!" Luna begs.

Santana chuckles. "Wear this," he says, tossing a white tank top at her. "And no bra."

Luna stands outside Stryker's apartment door wearing black leggings, a white tank top, and heeding Santana's advice she is not wearing a bra. She wore her favorite African print mask and her long black hair is in a high ponytail. Her neck is exposed, showing her small heart tattoo under her left earlobe. She knocks on the door and hears multiple locks unlock, then the door opens a crack and she sees him. Stryker Caine. He has the look of a California surfer minus the surfboard.

"Hey Luna," Stryker says, opening the door wider.

They are both wearing masks. Slowly blinking her long eyelashes, Luna tries to smile at him with her eyes.

"Come on in," Stryker says enthusiastically.

Luna suddenly feels shy, enters his apartment cautiously, and looks around. Stryker can't believe how luscious Luna looks. He sees the distinct impression of her hard nipples pressing against the fabric of her shirt and is instantly aroused.

"I came for the radio," Luna says, her voice shaking.

Oh, did you now, Stryker thinks to himself, wanting to throw her down on the couch and pull up her shirt, exposing her breasts.

"It's in the bedroom," Stryker says calmly.

He moves closer to her, thinking now he has full control and can easily make his move. Luna's heart is beating fast. She's thinking, Yes, please sweep me up in your muscular arms, take me into your bedroom and ravish me!

"Stay for a drink," Stryker says, interrupting her dramatic daydream of his hands all over her. *That was a statement not a question, he is taking charge.*

Stryker desperately wants to see Luna's beautiful face again. He imagines peeling off her mask and passionately kissing her right then and there. Impatiently he waits for her reply.

"Umm…" Luna begins.

Stryker senses Luna's hesitation. Before she can finish her sentence, he hands her a martini glass filled with a clear liquid and an olive on a toothpick.

"I made us Quarantinis," he says softly, almost in her ear.

Luna feels her body melting, her nipples erect with desire. Stryker walks across the room confidently and sits down on his couch—where the magic happens, Stryker thinks to himself. Luna will be my next conquest. He slyly takes off his mask, takes a long sip of his drink, and puts the martini glass down on the cluttered coffee table with a clank. Looking seductively at Luna, he pats the couch's cushion beside him.

"Come here and sit," Stryker says with authority.

Luna stands motionless. "Safety first," she says.

She chooses to sit down on the dingy armchair in the corner of Stryker's living room. *This is about six feet away. Thank heaven for social distancing.* Luna knows if she sits beside him on the couch, she will collapse into his arms.

Stryker is perplexed at her reaction, and he doesn't like it. *All women come after me, all the time! What is the matter with this woman?*

Stryker runs his fingers through his blond hair, exasperated. This is taking far too much effort. He's used to getting what he wants from women, whenever he wants it.

"I don't have a lot of time," Luna continues. "I have a ton of work waiting for me at home."

This is the truth. Luna needs to come up with a social media blitz that will blow the socks off her boss. How she will do this, Luna has no idea. She realizes Stryker is even more handsome up close. *His hair looks so soft, his eyes are so blue.* Luna needs to gain her composure, and a drink at this moment will help. She removes her mask and puts it in her lap. She raises the martini glass and with a quick nod to Stryker takes a gulp of her Quarantini.

Stryker thinks he has made a breakthrough watching Luna swig her drink. *A small breakthrough at that, but it's something.* He sees her brown full lips on the edge of the glass and wishes they were on his lips, kissing him. He studies her features. Luna has caramel colored skin, a slim nose, and doe-eyes.

"So, what do you do for fun?" Stryker asks.

"I dance," Luna says matter-of-factly.

Jeez it's like pulling teeth, Stryker thinks. Hopefully that drink will help her relax.

"What else do you enjoy…? Stryker asks with a slight innuendo in his voice. "Do you like live music?"

There's a pause before Luna responds. "Yeah, I like it, I guess…"

She puts her drink down. It's time to go, she thinks, before she gets too tipsy. Luna stands up anxiously, her mask in her hand.

"Well then, you should come check me out. I'm playing next Saturday at the Fury," Stryker says, and standing up also, he picks up a promotional postcard off the coffee table and hands it to her.

"Here are all the details," he says.

Luna takes the card, examining it quickly. "I have to go…the radio?" she says impatiently.

"Oh right. Let me get it," Stryker says and disappears into his bedroom.

Luna blows out a long breath, her heart racing. She wonders why she gave him such a hard time. But she knows why—she has an enormous crush on the infamous Stryker Caine.

Later that night Luna is back in her apartment at her computer with a glass of wine. She is texting with Santana while simultaneously Googling Stryker Caine's name.

SANTANA (TEXT)
So how did it go?

LUNA (TEXT)
Meh. Nothing happened. But my panties are all wet lol.

SANTANA (TEXT)
LMAO.

Luna quickly discovers results for the name Stryker Caine comes up all over Google. In Google images there are tons of photos of him. Headshots. Photos of him playing his guitar.

LUNA (TEXT)
Santana, Google him-his name is Stryker Caine!

SANTANA (TEXT)
K. brb.

Luna saves a few of the best photos of him onto her laptop. Then she scrolls through his profile on *Flikrz* @ strykercaine. Looking at his photos, she deciphers Stryker does not appear to have a girlfriend. Most of his profile photos are either selfies, or of him posing alone in a photo shoot. She finds it odd there are no photos of him with his family, no parents, or siblings. A true narcissist, Luna thinks.

SANTANA (TEXT)
Luna! He is so fucking hot!! Eggplant emoji. 4 fire emojis.

LUNA (TEXT)
I know! No one should be allowed to be that good looking!

SANTANA (TEXT)
So, what now?

LUNA (TEXT)
We are going to the Fury...next Saturday night, to hear him play.

SANTANA (TEXT)
Tongue emoji. Sounds like a plan.

It did. Luna thinks it sounds like a particularly good plan.

I need to find something juicy, Luna thinks. It's Thursday morning and she's working at home, trying to come up with a social media campaign to impress her boss, Meghan Kennedy, before the end of the week. *Ugh!* She has zero ideas and her brain is clogged up, constantly thinking about Stryker Caine. She looks at other fashion blogs for inspiration, yet she's left uninspired after trying for two hours.

A message alert pops up on the computer screen. It's a text from Darcy, the fashion editor at *Fashiondemic.*

"Hey Girl" it reads.

Luna hates that "Hey Girl" expression from Darcy. She wonders if Darcy uses it in communicating with White female colleagues or if it's just with her.

LUNA (TEXT)
Hi Darcy. What's up?

DARCY (TEXT)
I wanted to let you know the banner you made for YouTube is unacceptable.

LUNA (TEXT)
What's the problem with it, Darcy?

DARCY (TEXT)
It's blurry. I showed it to Meghan, and she agrees.

Luna is not fazed by Darcy's comment. Darcy is her nemesis who is constantly complaining about Luna to their boss behind her back. Luna doesn't reply to the text and goes to *Fashiondemic*'s YouTube website to see the banner for herself. Immediately she sees the YouTube banner posted isn't the one she made. *It must have been the intern. I am fucked.*

LUNA (TEXT)
I don't know where that version came from, but I didn't post it.

DARCY (TEXT)
Well are you going to fix it?

Luna doesn't have time for this nonsense, she's thinking about developing a social media campaign, not some banner on YouTube.

LUNA (TEXT)
Yeah. I am on it.

DARCY (TEXT)

When will it be done? This is the third time this week you have posted banners that are blurry.

Luna had tasked the social media banner creation to an intern. She presumes the intern must have been posting the banners to live sites without Luna's knowledge.

How though? Luna thinks, I didn't give him the password. Luna senses sabotage. And she is losing patience with Darcy's tone.

LUNA (TEXT)

I will take care of it.

Luna is not going to be bullied by Darcy. *I mean, who is she anyway?* She needs to get a hold of the intern and intercept Darcy's plan to go to Meghan. Luna is typing a text to the intern from her computer when her cell phone buzzes a high-pitched sound. Luna knows what the sound means—it's a COVID-25 text alert from the United States federal government.

This is an official message from the United States federal government: Please be aware that there has been a pocket of COVID-25 infection reported in the vicinity of 110th street to 116th street. If you think you have come into contact with individuals from this area, please immediately contact the nearest Contain Coronavirus Agency. Thank you for your continued efforts to stop the spread of COVID-25.

Stryker is lifting weights in his apartment. He stops what he's doing and listens to the COVID-25 alert twice on his cell phone. He's sure he hasn't been in that area and hopes Luna hasn't either. Since her visit to pick up his radio, Stryker finds himself frequently looking out his window, anticipating he would see Luna dancing on the rooftop. It was June 20th when he first saw her, the date of the summer solstice. The longest day and shortest night of the year. Stryker isn't sure that has any significance, but he does know it feels like an eternity since he last saw her.

It's Monday morning and Luna has finally come up with a new social media campaign for *Fashiondemic*, and she's excited to share it with Meghan in today's weekly staff meeting. Luna knows she missed Friday's deadline, but she's convinced it won't matter once she presents her idea. Luna feels it's that good!

The 123VideoMe call begins on time at 9:00 a.m., and Luna is preparing to give her presentation. There are ten people on the call. Luna doesn't recognize all the names, which makes her a little nervous. Nonetheless she speaks up at 9:05 a.m.

"Meghan, I am ready to present my social media campaign. It's called, 'A Passion for Fashion in Pandemic Times.'"

"Oh, don't bother Luna," Meghan says patronizingly. "Darcy is going to give a presentation on her social media campaign idea. I think her presentation will be better and more to the point."

Luna is shocked at being called out in a meeting by her boss. She's completely blindsided by the unexpected criticism in front of her colleagues. Luna hears Alex snickering in the background and is silent for the rest of the call, seething as Darcy gives her presentation.

At the conclusion of Darcy's presentation, Meghan says, "Well done Darcy!"

After the 123VideoMe call ends, Luna logs off. *I should have seen this coming. The signs were always there! I cannot believe I never recognized it!* Luna had refused to believe Darcy could act like a friend but truly not be a friend.

She hears a ding go off on her computer. It's an email meeting invitation from Meghan Kennedy. The meeting's in fifteen minutes.

"Ugh," Luna says aloud and goes into her kitchen to fix herself a cup of tea. *What a day this is turning out to be.*

Fifteen minutes later Luna is on the video call waiting for Meghan to appear on her computer screen. Luna doesn't know what to expect exactly but does know it's not going to be good. Meghan Kennedy suddenly appears on screen, sitting in what looks like her living room. Behind her are four massive windows that reach up to the ceiling. Shortly after the Pandemic intensified, Meghan moved from the Upper East Side to a Connecticut suburb. The furnishings in the room show Meghan clearly is well off. *She must live in a mansion with horses and a nanny.*

"Hello Luna," Meghan says dryly.

"Hi Meghan! How are you?" Luna says with as much fake enthusiasm as she can muster.

"I'm fine, Luna. Let me get to the point. For the past two months there has been negative feedback about your performance…"

Luna holds her breath. *Darcy! That undermining bitch!*

"Based on this, and the fact lately I have noticed you seem preoccupied… I'm afraid we are going to have to let you go," Meghan says without emotion.

"*Fashiondemic* will provide you with two weeks severance and health insurance through the end of the month."

Luna is dumbfounded. She has worked at *Fashiondemic* for the last five years. But what she's most worried about is her health insurance. COVID-25 requires U.S. citizens to get tested on a regular basis or face deportation to Canada. And God forbid should she catch the virus, how would she ever pay the hospital bills?

"But…" Luna hears herself say meekly.

"The decision is made Luna. I will pay you through the rest of the week. However today is your last day with *Fashiondemic*."

"My assistant will mail you a preaddressed FedEx box for you to return your laptop." Meghan looks blankly at Luna.

"Ok," Luna says.

I mean, what can I say? I am not going to beg for my job.

Meghan clicks off the meeting. Luna sits shell shocked. She wants to throw her laptop against the wall.

"Fuck!" she says. "Fuck me."

CHAPTER 3

STRYKER THINKS BACK to his experience at Burning Man in 2019. An accumulation of chance encounters that would change the course of his life forever, starting with this trip to the dessert. It's nightfall and The Man was burning in the desert. Stryker watched the eight-foot wooden figure engulfed in flames while standing beside hundreds of people he didn't know but somehow felt close to in those moments. His buddies were elsewhere on the Playa—drinking, dancing, or doing drugs in the camp. He didn't know, and he didn't care. Stryker had come to Burning Man 2019 as a "Sparkle Pony" with the intent of having mass amounts of sex with beautiful women, doing mushrooms, and listening to some music. While the residents of Black Rock City existed on only their own wits and self-reliance, Stryker and his cohorts languished in luxury accommodations in a turnkey plug and play camp.

He'd arrived at Burning Man three days ago, the last year for the event before the virus hit in 2020. Stryker spent the first day indulging in all forms of debauchery he could find. Each day was 100 degrees on the Playa, dust storms would come out of nowhere and were so extreme and blinding the sand felt like tiny harsh pellets when it hit his skin. On the second day Stryker found himself deep in the Playa, thirsty as hell, and nowhere near his posh camp. He was covered in sand dust and miserable. He decided to go in search of water, leaving behind the two half naked women he was with. Gorgeous women at Burning Man were at his disposal. He knew he could easily find two or three more later on.

"Hey man, looks like you could use a drink," a bearded man said, tossing a bottle of water at him. The man was sitting in a folding chair.

Stryker caught the bottle and drank the entire contents before he said anything. He could use about three more bottles of water, he thought, and eyed the case of spring water beside the man's feet.

"Go ahead, take some," the man offered.

"Thanks," Stryker said, taking a bottle in each hand.

Stryker closed his eyes while he drank the water, the thumping of the non-stop electronic music in his ears. People were riding on bicycles everywhere, and strange vehicles called art cars were traversing the vast flat desert around the two of them. Stryker sat on the ground next to the man and finished consuming the water. After he was rehydrated, he looked more closely at the man. He was wrapped in a blanket and resembled a prophet. His green eyes were kind, and he seemed completely at peace.

"I'm Malcolm."

"I'm Stryker," Stryker said.

"First time?" Malcolm asked.

"Yeah."

"Your body will adapt after a few days," Malcolm told him.

Stryker wanted to be back in the comfort of his opulent camp. But he wasn't sure where that was. It was late at night, or almost morning, or so he thought, but he had no way of knowing what time it was either.

"I was just about to go to the Jazz Café, do you want to join me?"

"Sure, sure," Stryker said.

He followed behind Malcolm to his mutant vehicle. It looked like an insect—its side panels iridescent like the skin of a beetle, the colors a blend of a shiny blue-purple, green, and orange. The top of the auto was a dome in the shape of a cockroach head with two thick black antennas protruding out of it. Around the borders of the roof were hundreds of rusty nail heads. On the front of the car were two giant operating room lamps with red bulbs. It looked sinister and Stryker questioned whether he should get inside. He hesitated then climbed in and Malcolm took off, driving it across the playa.

As the vehicle approached the jazz camp, Stryker saw the infamous giant neon sign "Jazz Café" outside it. Malcolm parked, and they hurried inside to avoid the oppressive elements. Inside the tent, the audience reclined on bean bag chairs, couches, and rugs on the floor. Most people had their eyes closed. Malcolm and Stryker went to the bar and ordered Irish coffees. Stryker stayed and listened for hours to the melodic sound of the musicians and the breakout solos of a man on a trumpet improvising a Miles Davis song. For the remainder of Burning Man, the Jazz Café became Stryker's sanctuary, a daily ritual where he took refuge every evening.

Stryker felt a rush of emotions. He couldn't explain how the sounds sent shivers through his body as the music rose, exploded, and tapered off. He realized up until now he had led a life of very little meaning. Over the long nights of deep conversations, he slowly developed a kinship with the people around him. They talked about musical styles and techniques. Stryker vowed when he left Burning to stop wasting his time and to pursue his dream of becoming a true musician. As he stood watching the Burning Man fall to pieces in glowing embers in the night sky, Stryker cleansed his mind and began his journey to find freedom in the music he loved so much.

CHAPTER 4

SANTANA HAS ALREADY heard about the club, The Fury. It's a seedy bar with a stage, Santana thinks, not a dance club. He's waiting for Luna outside the entrance. He has his certification papers to prove he's virus free but is worried about the clientele inside. Musicians don't wear masks and neither do customers. Bars are considered safe havens and have limited seating with tables spaced far apart. Still, Santana knows there's a risk he could catch COVID-25, but he's there to support his best friend Luna. He also wants to see the handsome Stryker Caine in person.

Santana sees Luna up the street, walking toward him. She's depressed about recently getting fired from her job, and he hopes this night will be a distraction from all of that. She's wearing a black low-cut sundress, sexy platform sandals, and a black silk mask.

"Hey Santana," Luna says. "Are you ready to get your drink on?"

She's half kidding, but she's open to the idea. Luna has even stopped thinking about Stryker. It was Santana who reminded her about tonight's performance. He probably has a boy crush, Luna thinks to herself.

"Hi Luna, you look beautiful as always," Santana says, ignoring her comment.

Once they are successfully inside, their temperatures and IDs having been checked at the door, Luna and Santana are told to remove their masks. The Fury is dimly lit and has a western vibe with hay scattered on the floor. The room is packed with young men and women sitting at tables in front of the stage. People are having loud conversations, and their hearty laughter fills the air. Luna and Santana sit down at a table in the back of the room. That's where Luna insists they sit, she didn't want Stryker to see her. They order Southern Mules off the drink menu and settle into their wooden chairs. Santana can see Luna's in a funk but doesn't blame her, knowing she just lost her job and finding a new one in the Pandemic is near impossible.

"Boo, that job was beneath you anyway," Santana says sympathetically.

"Yeah, it was," Luna says. She's thinking of Darcy's face, her shoulders stiffening as she clenches her hands into fists. *That bitch!*

"You are so much better than those people," Santana continues. "Have you thought about going out on your own? Running your own social media campaigns? I mean, you are so good at it..."

Santana remembers before the Pandemic when he taught Zumba Master Classes. Luna did his social media marketing, and her efforts doubled his following on all his social accounts.

"Hmm," Luna says. Changing the subject, she comments, "There are sure a lot of people in here. Risking their lives to hear some music…"

She studies the paper flyer on the table. It reads—*The Fury proudly presents an evening with Stryker Caine.* She looks around anxiously as the audience begins chanting, "We want Stryker Caine! We want Stryker Caine!" Luna perks up as she's surprised Stryker pulls in such a large and enthusiastic crowd.

Stryker is backstage making small talk with Logan, the drummer, waiting for his cue. And there it is, Stryker thinks as he hears the familiar sound of his fans shouting his name.

"Damn, they love you," Logan says.

"Come on! Let's get it," Stryker says in an exaggerated baritone voice.

Stryker is wearing a plaid western shirt. The shirt has the classic two front pocket flaps with silver snaps. Logan is about Stryker's age, in his late twenties, and has a mop of brown hair that covers his ears. Stryker identifies with Logan. *Drummers get a whole lot of females.* He's sure he will also get some of that attention tonight. He has quite a following with the ladies.

"Ladies and gentlemen…" the MC announces, "what you all have been waiting for…Stryker Caine!"

The audience erupts into applause as Stryker struts out on stage with conviction.

"Thank you. Thank you," Stryker says with genuine gratitude.

He sits down on the stool and begins playing his acoustic guitar. The audience quiets. There are a group of pretty girls sprinkled throughout the front row looking at him with adoration.

He plays two familiar songs, "Here and Now" by Kenny Chesney and "Gabrielle" by Brett Eldredge. His voice has a slight rasp in it, and he smiles from time to time at the audience. His singing voice is tantalizing and seductive and combined with his handsome features he's irresistible. No one in the crowd can take their eyes off of him. Stryker is captivating.

Shortly into his third song, a man in the audience yells out, "Quarantina!" Soon after, an attractive woman cries out, "Quarantina!" When two more yelps from the crowd shout, "Quarantina!" Stryker stops playing his guitar and slowly grins.

"Here's one you all may know," Stryker says in a sultry whisper.

He begins strumming his guitar and singing.

Did you fall down, did you hit the ground or did you make your way around?

Qua-ran-tina, Qua-ran-tina…

When the entire audience sings in unison, the words "*Qua-ran-tina, Qua-ran-tina,*" Luna feels goosebumps go up and down her bare arms. Stryker's voice and words are so arousing. Santana's eyes are glued to the stage. Stryker continues singing the next two verses.

Were you paralyzed? Were you hypnotized? Were you petrified by

Qua-ran-tina, Qua-ran-tina…

The crowd sings the chorus, passionately swaying to the music.

Did you scream and shout, did you thrash about and wonder how you got to

Qua-ran-tina, Qua-ran-tina

When humankind fell far behind this frightful time were you blinded by

Qua-ran-tina, Qua-ran-tina

Luna listens to the lyrics—Stryker's voice delivers so much emotion.

And if you made it through would it occur to you your life is now just a

Qua-ran-tina, Qua-ran-tina

Stryker ends the song. The audience cheers, a man whistles, and the women in the front row give him a standing ovation.

"Wow, that was something," Santana says.

Luna is silent. She's spellbound. This experience has left a lasting impression, and she knows Stryker is a star undiscovered. He needs to be famous.

Stryker ends his set and before he can put his guitar down and stand up, he's swarmed by women from the audience. There are a few men as well who are hanging back, somewhat embarrassed they are also fans. Everyone has their cell phones out, taking pictures and video.

"I never heard about this guy," Santana says, somewhat mystified.

"You and me both. He should promote himself better on social media," Luna says absently.

"Why don't you do it Luna?"

"Do what?" she says in confusion.

"Why don't you promote him on social media," Santana

encourages. "You are great at that, and it would give you a reason to get close to him."

"Close to him? I can't even get his attention. He has so many girls!" Luna says, dismissing the idea. "I am going to find the ladies' room, be right back." She heads across the room.

Stryker is overcome by the pretty women around him. He loves being adored and can barely form sentences as everyone asks questions or leans against him, taking selfies. Then he notices an alluring woman at the back of the room talking with a handsome Hispanic man. *Is that Luna? She did come to hear me play! But with some guy?... It must be her date, or worse yet her boyfriend.* He watches her intently then sees her walking toward the hallway where the bathrooms are. *I must do something!* Stryker stands up, urgently wanting to follow her.

"Excuse me ladies," Stryker says and takes long strides across the room after Luna.

The hallway is dark, Luna can barely find her way to the ladies' room. Suddenly she feels two hands on her waist from behind. "Luna," a male voice says in her ear. She recognizes the voice. It's Stryker and he spins her around. Pushing her against the wall Stryker kisses her lustfully. Luna feels her body melting at his touch. She kisses him back intensely, her hands on his head, touching his soft blond hair. Stryker pushes the sides of her dress upward. He feels Luna is not wearing underwear. In her peripheral vision Luna sees a figure standing at the end of the hallway. Stryker sees it too, stops kissing her, and takes a step backward. He's still holding Luna's midsection with both hands. He did not want to let her go.

Luna sees it's Santana.

Santana turns around self-consciously and walks in the other direction until he hears Luna's frantic voice. "Santana, wait!" Luna says, flustered, adjusting her sundress.

"I have to go," she says to Stryker and hurries down the dark hallway after Santana.

Watching her disappear down the corridor, Stryker thinks, Dammit! I let her slip through my fingers again. And now I have competition? Stryker has never had to compete for a woman's attention before. *Who is this idiot she's with?*

CHAPTER 5

IT'S BEEN FOUR days since Stryker and Luna's intimate kiss was interrupted. Stryker is beside himself. He can't think of anything else. The way Luna's lips tasted, how she kissed him back. He's going over and over it in his mind. *She should be mine by now! Not with some guy in skinny jeans.* He tries to figure out what he must do to get her. He's never had to pursue a woman like this before. He's always the object of affection. The stud. To his surprise, he hears a knock on his door.

That's strange, I'm not expecting anyone. "Who's there?" he says through the door.

"It's Luna."

Stryker looks through the doors' peephole. Luna stands there wearing a mask.

It is Luna! She's come to her senses and wants me now more than ever.

"One second," Stryker says.

Not wanting to appear too eager, he takes his time putting on the blue surgical mask from a box he keeps by the door. *This is how it should be, the woman comes after me.*

Stryker unlocks the four locks on his apartment door, all except for the chain lock. *I am not going to make this easy for her. After all, I've gone through a lot. The wondering, the worrying that Luna is already taken. That I have lost my touch.* He looks at her through the crack of the doorway. *She's stunning, even in casual clothes.* Luna is wearing white cut off shorts and a coral paisley midriff top.

"I have a proposition for you," she says.

Stryker closes the door and removes the chain lock. He opens the door completely and gives Luna a flirtatious look, scanning her body from head to toe.

Luna thinks, Oh my God, he is so irresistible.

"Come in Luna. Come in."

Luna steps inside, and Stryker closes the door behind her. Before Stryker can say a word, Luna begins speaking. "A business proposition," she says coyly, "I have a business proposition for you."

Deflated, Stryker feels like someone just poured cold water on his head. He is totally unfamiliar with being teased by a woman.

"Oh yeah...what is it?" he says, visibly annoyed.

Luna knows she's in the catbird seat. *I am in control.*

"May I sit down?" she says, playfully looking at the couch in Stryker's living room.

"Sure, sure," he says. Admiring Luna's slim frame, he desperately wants to touch her and pull her close to him.

I had to practically beg her to sit down the last time she was here. What the hell is going on?

"Would you like a drink?" Stryker, still taken off guard,

now remembers it's only 10 a.m. Correcting himself he says, "Coffee? Tea?"

Stryker has neither of these. He is so discombobulated at this point he knows he would offer Luna just about anything. He doesn't like being in a position of weakness in front of any woman and especially not in front of Luna who he is thirsting for.

"No, but thank you."

Luna removes her mask so he can hear her better. Stryker does as well, detaching his mask while looking directly into her eyes. He's curious about her "business proposal" but knows whatever it is it will give him a reason to spend time with her.

"You said you were here about business?"

"Oh right, yes…" Luna loses her train of thought. She's fantasizing about when they made out. *He looks so delicious.* She wants to throw herself at him, she desires him so much.

"I'm…I'm an influencer," Luna says, stumbling over her words slightly.

"A-hunh…and?" Stryker is anxious to learn what Luna is getting at.

"Your performance at The Fury was quite memorable."

"It's always like that for me when I play," Stryker says with some conceit.

"Right. Exactly. You are clearly a star in the making." Luna pauses for effect. "But you need help to reach that next level," Luna affirms.

Stryker smiles and sits next to Luna on the couch. He's careful not to sit too close for fear she may jump up and run out of his apartment like she did the last time. He imagines touching her exposed thigh, rubbing his hand up and down in a comforting way. She seems so nervous, Stryker thinks.

"So, what did you have in mind?" Stryker leans forward with temptation.

Luna's heart beats rapidly. Her body begins to tingle from having Stryker sitting right beside her. It's almost more than she can take. She wants him to force her down on the couch and kiss her wildly. *Is he going to kiss me again?* The sexual tension builds, and Luna doesn't know what to do. Focus! Focus! Luna thinks and leans back away from him. "As I was saying, I'm an influencer…and at the moment I'm in between engagements so this would be the perfect time for me to promote you on social…for me to widen my net of clients."

"Oh, you mean like Kylie Jenner?"

"Yes! Exactly like that. You would be the talent I would promote."

"How much would it cost me?"

Stryker isn't concerned about the cost and thinks how cute it is Luna has come up with the entire idea. He looks at her taut stomach, shiny with small beads of perspiration. He wants to lay her down on the couch and lick her abdomen. Then slowly unzip her white cutoff shorts and pull them down over her hips, undressing her. He wants to see the lower half of her body again. Her honey colored skin he exposed the night they kissed.

"It's complimentary. A proof of concept showcasing my social media marketing skills," Luna assures him. "It would help me get more clients and create a social buzz for you."

Stryker still doesn't know where that guy he saw her

with fits into all of this. *Is she already off the market? Is that the reason why she's so standoffish?* Stryker first needs to know, *Is this a package deal? Does that guy come along with this offer?* He needs that bit of information before he commits to anything. He doesn't like seeing Luna with another man for even a minute.

"Well, maybe…I need time to think it over. What's your number? Give me your card."

This isn't the answer Luna expected. She thought Stryker would just say yes because he's attracted to her. That he wants her as much as she wants him. Luna tries to hide her disappointment as she gets up from the couch.

"I forgot to bring them." Luna is lying. She doesn't have any business cards.

Stryker senses he's hurt Luna's feelings by not immediately accepting her offer. He has to make this right. He didn't mean to offend her. That's the furthest thing from his mind. It's true Stryker lusts for her, but it's more than that. He has never had this feeling of anticipation for any woman before. Luna is so sumptuous, yet so unattainable.

"Ok, no worries. I'll just put your number in my phone," Stryker says. He holds his phone, waiting to get her information.

Luna gazes at him. Stryker has his head down, waiting for her to speak. *His chest is so broad, I bet he has a six pack underneath that t-shirt.* She's losing the control she thought she had over him.

"555-329-7735," Luna says shyly. "I have to go."

Stryker stands up. Luna loves how tall he is. *He must be at least 6'2".* She would need to stand on her tiptoes if she were to kiss him again. Luna's insides quiver, but she can't let him see her so vulnerable.

"You always have to go," Stryker says. It's true she's always saying this to him. He wants her to stay but feels her drifting away yet again. "Well, we should really discuss this further… Over dinner, what do you think Luna?"

Stryker has never been rejected by a woman before and hopes it won't be today. Not by the woman he dreams about.

Luna loves hearing him speak her name. *His voice is so sexy*. Yet she doesn't respond.

"A business meeting…" Stryker finds himself saying.

"It would be a business meeting," he clarifies.

"A business meeting," Luna repeats back to him.

"Yes. A business meeting." *God, I want to grab her and tear her clothes off!*

Luna is overjoyed at the thought of seeing Stryker again. Even if it's not a date, Luna says to herself. Then she says out loud, "Ok."

"Ok then, on Saturday around 7:30, I will text you the details," Stryker says.

Luna likes the way Stryker is taking control. That he is telling her what to do. Like the night he grabbed her and kissed her so passionately.

"Ok, then," Luna says meekly. She opens the door to Stryker's apartment and lets herself out. Once on the other side she lets out a long sigh. She smiles and heads home.

ঌ

STRYKER (TEXT)
Hi Luna. I sent a UFetchr for you it will arrive at 7:30 p.m.

LUNA (TEXT)
Hi. OK, I will be ready.

STRYKER (TEXT)
I made reservations for us. 8:00 p.m. at Five Madison Park.

LUNA (TEXT)
OK, see you then.

STRYKER (TEXT)
OK

He sent a car for me and *we are going to Five Madison Park! One of the most expensive restaurants in Manhattan. He is going all out.*

Later that evening Luna's getting dressed, trying to decide between a red dress with a deep V front or a black dress that is equally sexy. Red! she decides. Feeling like "Pretty Woman" in the movie, Luna wriggles into it, pulling the dress over her mane of black curls. It's tight in all the right places and Luna looks delectable. She puts on her red bottom heels and looking into her vanity mirror she puts on her makeup. She carefully applies eyeliner, drawing sultry cat eye wings enhancing her innocent, wide-eyed look. Her skin is smooth and even toned so foundation isn't necessary. She swishes red lipstick on her full brown lips, and she's ready to go. She's rubbing her lips together, spreading lipstick evenly on the top and bottom when her phone vibrates.

It's a text from UFetchr informing her the self-driving car is two minutes away. Luna hurries to the lobby and sees the black BMW waiting in front of her building. The car is immaculate and disinfected inside. She has no worries settling into the car's backseat, she did not even need to wear her mask. *I mean I'm going to Five Madison Park. There the virus doesn't even exist!*

The car arrives at the restaurant at 7:55 p.m., and she sees Stryker lingering patiently on the sidewalk. He's dressed in a gray suit with a black button-down shirt. He looks so European and rich, Luna thinks.

"Good evening Luna, you look beautiful," Stryker says, opening the car's door.

Luna swings her bare long legs out of the car and stands facing Stryker. The red dress hugs her body, and his thoughts wander to their previous encounter when he lifted her dress ever so slightly revealing she wore nothing underneath. He wants to take her hand and guide her inside the restaurant's doorway. Then Stryker remembers this is a "business meeting" and instead he holds out his arm, gesturing to Luna to step ahead of him.

As soon as they walk inside, they are both tested for COVID-25 via a shiny silver testing machine next to the hostesses stand. The hostess is a pretty brunette in a black form fitting dress. Stryker speaks through his mask and gives her his last name.

"Caine," he says. "Party of two."

"Temperature check," she says, waving a magnetic wand in front of each of their foreheads.

"You passed." She puts the wand down on the podium. "Come on through."

In front of Luna is what looks like a metal detector used at airports. Luna turns a puzzled look to the hostess.

"Come on through," the hostess says again.

Luna steps inside, and a sudden burst of mist surrounds her. Startled, she shudders. She can barely see, yet she has the sense to step forward out from underneath it. Stryker quickly follows, gets sprayed, and steps through the apparatus without missing a beat.

"It's an antimicrobial chemical mist," he explains. "We won't need to wear masks for twenty-four hours."

"Oh!" Luna says, trying to contain a cough.

"They also pump it throughout the vents in the restaurant, so we are completely safe from the virus." Stryker rubs his thumb and index finger together, signifying big money.

Luna has read about electrostatic spraying on the internet. That it's used at luxury hotels and celebrity mansions. She thought it was a myth, but now she knows otherwise. Outside the dining room is a basket simply marked "Masks" where they both drop their masks. Luna is dazzled by the restaurant's décor. The massive interior is made entirely of tan marble and the ceilings are at least twenty feet high. Fancy chandeliers glow from above as they're led to a table in a secluded corner and seated.

"This is quite extravagant…how do you afford it?" Luna says, stunned.

"I know a couple of the waiters who work here," Stryker

says nonchalantly, whipping the white napkin into the air, laying it down on his lap. "They comp me all the time."

If she only knew, Stryker thinks to himself. He's ecstatic he's impressed her. Two attentive waiters with slicked-back hair take their order. Stryker orders a Manhattan and Luna orders a glass of Perrier Jouet. While they sample exquisite appetizers, Stryker gets right to the point. "Shall we get down to business?"

"Yes, let's," Luna says matter-of-factly. "Have you had time to consider my offer?" She lifts her glass to her lips. "I'm only available for a short time. I'm sure other people will want my services."

Stryker knows she's bluffing but indulges her nonetheless. "Well only the best for the best," he says in a cavalier tone while mesmerized by her beauty.

At this point he would give almost anything to be with her, including letting her manage his music career image, not that he needs the money or the fame. No longer hearing her speak, his eyes slowly drift from her face to her well-endowed cleavage. *The front of her dress almost reaches her belly button.* He longs to see her stomach again. Stryker noticed her navel was pierced when he last saw her. *That's downright sexy.* Stryker is aroused at the sight of her brown skin and feels the front of his trousers getting tighter and tighter, imagining Luna naked. There is so much sexual tension between them, they can't take their eyes off each other.

He's so overconfident, especially not having much of a career. He just plays in some dive club, Luna thinks. Maybe I should knock him down a few pegs.

"Anyway, that guy. That guy you were with, is he your business partner?" Stryker asks

"What guy?"

"The guy at The Fury you were with last Saturday."

Luna wants to laugh out loud, *Oh, he's jealous.* She finds it endearing that Stryker has some vulnerabilities. "Nooo. That's my best friend, Santana. And romantically he prefers a different gender."

Whew, that's a relief, Stryker thinks.

"So, are we in business or not?" Luna asks delicately.

"Yes, I *mean* business," Stryker says, extending his hand across the table for Luna to shake.

Luna shakes his hand—and can't hold back a smile. This is the first time they have touched since their steamy kiss in the hallway. Stryker holds her hand a moment longer, looking lustfully into her eyes. Luna gently pulls her hand away and shyly sits back in her comfy chair. Stryker thinks Luna is so cute when her shyness shows. *It means she's as attracted to me as I am to her.*

Carried by two waiters, their chic inspired food arrives at the table. Luna marvels at how well her meal is plated. It looks like a piece of art, she thinks, pushing her fork into the truffles.

"I'm so hungry," Stryker says. He's hungry for Luna and wants her to know.

"Me too," Luna says.

Stryker wants to figure out how to find her current romantic status without coming off as nosy. "So how is dating for you in the Pandemic?" he asks, wishing he could stroke her bare thigh under the table.

Dating is nonexistent for Luna. She wants him to know she's available but not desperate. "It's okay. What about you?"

"Not much. I'm all about self-care when the mood hits me. I use *Friendneedz.com*." You know the site where you video chat each other. Plus, it's the only safe alternative." Stryker winks at her.

Luna thinks of him masturbating and blushes. *At least he practices safe social distancing.* She has been doing the same thing, masturbating every night this week. Each time before making herself climax she imagined the night they kissed. She fantasied about Stryker sliding her black sun-dress dress up, fingering her beneath it. Tonight, she's again unrestricted. She feels herself getting wet with excitement and gracefully uncrosses her bare legs then crosses them the opposite way beneath the dinner table.

Stryker watches her shifting in her chair and pictures him on his knees, spreading her legs and slowly putting his tongue between her thighs. He would make her body shiver in ecstasy with the whole room watching. *I must get her back to my place immediately so I can feel every part of her body.*

Getting up from the table now would be difficult, especially since she's left a lasting impression from inside his gray trousers. Instead he holds his hand up and beckons the waiter over, hoping his erection will eventually calm itself.

"Yes sir?" the waiter asks.

Luna is hot with desire from their heated conversation. She wants to fan herself with her hand to compose herself. Instead she lets out what she thought was a quiet sigh.

Stryker hears her and sees her eyes are on him. *She is feeling it too.* He knows they need to leave now.

"Put this on my tab," Stryker says to the waiter.

"Yes of course, so good to see you again, sir."

Luna is impressed at the clout he has here.

As soon as the waiter is gone, Stryker grasps Luna's hand, drawing her to her feet. "Let's go back to my place and continue our conversation," he says.

"Let's go," Luna feels herself saying.

Stryker lets Luna walk in front of him. Her dress exposes her back, and Stryker's eyes admires her as she swings her hips from side to side. The UFetchr, as Stryker has instructed, is waiting on the street outside the restaurant. Luna is a little surprised by this but is caught up in the moment and doesn't question it. They quickly climb inside and as soon as the car door shuts, Stryker pushes his body against Luna, kissing her madly. The self-driving car speeds off into the night, heading to Stryker's apartment.

Stryker has finally made his move and now he's alone with Luna. She is overcome with the anticipation of touching Stryker's bare skin—she can barely catch her breath. Once they're inside his apartment, Stryker unzips Luna's dress from behind, and it falls to the floor around her feet. She is completely naked. Stryker kisses her neck with an open mouth while putting his hands on her breasts, cupping them in each palm. He pinches her nipples, and Luna feels Stryker's tongue on her neck.

"I want to see you," Stryker says. "I want to see your body."

He suddenly picks her up. Luna's torso is on his shoulder with her head hanging down his back. Stryker carries her into the bedroom. He wants to make love to her, not like the parade of women he has sex with on his couch.

In a fluid motion, he slides her off his shoulder onto the bed. Luna bounces a bit on the mattress, her black curls in her face. She brushes them out her eyes. She's excited Stryker is so aggressive and wonders what he'll do next. The room has a warm white glow from a small lamp on the night table. Stryker quickly removes his shoes and slowly unbuttons his black shirt to reveal his well-defined abdomen and clean-shaven chest.

"Get on your knees," he commands.

Luna obeys, and rolling over she gets up on her knees on the bed.

"Your body is so beautiful," Stryker says, tossing his shirt in the corner.

Stryker slowly unzips his gray trousers. He's wearing tight fitting boxers that he quickly removes, displaying his massive erection. Luna is pleased at the size of him. Stryker, free from his clothes, now naked, thrusts himself inside Luna's mouth. She gladly accepts, taking as much of him as she can. Stryker gently grabs the back of her head, forcing himself deeper and deeper inside her mouth. Luna doesn't want him to finish yet. She wants to feel him inside her when he ejaculates, so she pushes herself back, flipping herself around so he can enter her from behind. Luna feels Stryker push himself inside her, and she moans. Stryker is on the verge, and the motion of him is just the right amount of pressure to make her climax. She is so close. He reaches around her thigh and with his right hand massages her in just the right place. It's too much for her. Waves of pleasure cascade through her body with Stryker finishing at the same time. They both collapse onto the bed, fulfilled like never before.

CHAPTER 6

IT'S 10:45 A.M. on Sunday, and Santana is getting ready to teach his Zumba livestream class on *Phit.live* when Luna FaceTimes him.

"Hey Boo!" Santana says, knowing last night was her big date with Stryker. He's more than curious, but seeing Luna beam, he has his answer immediately. Santana has never seen her smile so hard.

"Aah, it must have been some date," he teases. "So did you finally get some?"

"Oh my God, Santana! Stryker took such good care of me. In and out of bed," Luna says gleefully.

Her eyes are sparkling, her voice breathy. Santana knows Luna must of gotten fucked good. "So how big is it?"

"Oh my God, so big, and so thick…I keep thinking about it!"

Santana has not seen her act like this before, so forthcoming with gritty details. He's happy for her but knows he has to ask. "What about the virus?"

"That's the thing. We both got tested at the restaurant

and then got sprayed with that anti-microbiological thing where you are not infectious for a full twenty-four hours."

"Jesus! You must have fucked like rabbits."

"We did! We did! Three times and again in the morning…he's such a stud."

Santana has read about the anti-microbial spray on the dark web. He knows it's hard to come by and costs big money just for a little bit. *To have their whole bodies sprayed? That must have costs thousands!* "That must have cost a few grand each. This guy's a musician? " Santana says suspiciously.

"Oh, and the dinner at Five Madison Park was beyond compare! Stryker had so much clout there, we had two separate waiters serving us."

Santana feels he has to say something, even if it hurts his best friend's feelings.

"That man has got something going on Luna," Santana says. "He's not some poor musician…is he a drug dealer?"

"No, he's not a drug dealer," Luna says in annoyance. "He knows people who work at that restaurant…we got comped. Just be happy for me Santana," she says, her voice cracking.

"I *am* very happy for you Luna, you deserve to be treated like a princess, princess," Santana says, tilting his head with an affectionate expression, making the heart sign with his hands.

"Thank you. Now I have to get busy promoting him all over the place. Love you…"

"Love you too," Santana says back to her.

Luna clicks off the call. She's silent for a moment and

shuts her eyes, shaking her head a tiny bit to shrug off Santana's words.

"Time to get to work," Luna says aloud, popping open her laptop.

Stryker is on his couch, practicing songs on his guitar, reminiscing about last night with Luna. He wonders if he's finally in love. At least he's in deep infatuation. He loved waking up with Luna after spooning with her naked body all night. He loved the way her brown eyes shimmered when he was on top of her, inside her. For the first time in his life, Stryker is off balance because of a woman.

Luna gets right to work and uses the next three days to put her social promotion plan to work. She spends hours on *WorkDawgs.com* searching through her connections from when she worked at *Fashiondemic* for *the* Meghan Kennedy. Having worked as a social media manager for a top online publication, she amassed a bevy of connections of influential bloggers, influencers, and social media strategists. She knows the key to making her digital marketing plan succeed is for her to make every personalized invitation she extends seem like it's a privilege to see Stryker Caine perform. That *she,* a prolific social media manager for *Fashiondemic*, is doing them a great service by having been selected to be the first to hear such a star in the making play.

Luna's sexy WorkDawgs profile photo works for her as well. When she direct messages bloggers and influencers, male and female, they immediately DM her back, asking her out for drinks. Instead Luna entices them, and then seals the deal with, "Drinks with you sometime? Maybe. Btw on July 30th 9 p.m. I will be at The Fury, swing on by and hear a Stryker Caine set. You won't be disappointed 😉!"

The social media strategists she contacts are not as easily swayed, and Luna has to get creative and barter services—if they come see Stryker Caine perform, in return she'll mention their client in *Fashiondemic*'s Blog and on *@Flikrz*. Little do they know she's been fired from *Fashiondemic* and has no claim to them or their blog. Then it gets personal for Luna, and she's forced to do something she hates. She knows she will have to do it, to get the right person in the club for Stryker's performance.

Luna combs through her rival, Darcy Brooks', social media contacts and reaches out to the most important ones, using Darcy's name as an introduction. She's disgusted having to do this and also wonders if Darcy will catch wind of her scheme and call her out on it on social media. She despises Darcy. If not for her, Luna knows she would still have a job at *Fashiondemic*. Success is the best revenge, Luna thinks. Drastic times, call for drastic measures.

Luna is elated. By Wednesday evening everything is in place for Stryker's premiere at The Fury. She happily texts Stryker with a status update.

LUNA (TEXT)
Hey stud, (eggplant emoji)

STRYKER (TEXT)
Luna.

LUNA (TEXT)
Everything is all set, make July 30th your best performance ever!

STRYKER (TEXT)
That's great. When do we have sex again? You are so hot!

LUNA (TEXT)
Tonight. xoxo (tongue emoji)

Luna is inside The Fury. It's 7:30 p.m., the night of Stryker's big event. She's running on adrenaline—so excited to see her social media marketing plan in action. She wears a sheer white button-down blouse, a distressed denim mini skirt, and nude high heeled wedge sandals. She's adoringly watching Stryker on center stage, sitting on a stool. He's adjusting, tuning the guitar's scale. Every so often he lifts his head and smiles at her. Then he shakes his glossy head of blond hair out of his eyes and goes back to playing notes. Luna can't believe she has been with Stryker exclusively for three and a half weeks. They have been alternating days sleeping at each other's apartments. Each evening they have sex as if their lives depend on it. Luna has never experienced so much pleasure. She has fallen hard for Stryker Caine.

Pleased with the turnout, she spends the next two hours seating her guests in the VIP section of the dusty bar. Fashionistas, bloggers, influencers, most of the people she invited showed up. As the lights go down and Stryker comes on stage, Luna is already filming with her camera. Stryker receives a thunderous round of applause. The VIP section takes notice and looks up from their cell phones. Once he begins singing, they're fixated by his hypnotic voice.

After two songs Stryker begins playing "Quarantina" with the crowd enthusiastically chanting the chorus, "Qua-ran-tina, Qua-ran-tina." By this time everyone in the packed club has begun to break loose with excitement. The audience is rowdy while the social media kings and queens Luna invited are live streaming Stryker's performance. Others are taking video clips and uploading them onto *Flikrz* and Facebooks' stories. Luna loves seeing social media spread like wildfire right in front of her. Her plan is working!

Toward the end of the show one of the influencers rushes up to Luna asking, "Isn't that Jackson Caine?"

Perplexed, Luna replies, "It's...he's Stryker Caine..."

"Oh...well, that's his middle name. Yeah, I knew him as Jackson Caine. His father is Merritt Caine...he owns Caine Financial."

Caine Financial? The multi-billion dollar global technology company? Merritt Caine is on this year's short list to becoming a trillionaire by 2030.

"This is going to make great press. Hello TMZ," the influencer exclaims, taking another picture with his cell phone.

Luna stares at the rambunctious audience, then stares at Stryker, then she turns back, looking blankly at the influencer standing beside her.

"Qua-ran-tina, Qua-ran-tina! That song *is* kind of catchy, isn't it?"

When Stryker's set ends he leaves the stage, waving at the audience who are on their feet howling and cheering. Luna is mortified and feels the blood rushing to her head. Her temples throb. She sees the VIP section animated in conversation and tweeting furiously. She worries they will come up to talk with her about the show and wants to bolt from the room to avoid all contact.

How could he keep this from me? Being one of the richest men on the planet's son. Luna feels betrayed and like a fool for trusting him. *Stryker could have gained all this attention on his own. He never needed to play in some dive bar, WTF!*

Luna honestly believed she'd finally found the right guy that she never knew even existed. Now everything is suddenly being pulled out from beneath her. Stryker is not the person he portrayed himself to be. This is a new level of betrayal. His deception has gone on for weeks with her and she's devastated! Such dishonesty from a man is something Luna has never experienced before. *I will never get over this!* Fuming, near tears she sends him a text. Before any VIPs can approach with questions about Stryker's performance, Luna darts out the back door of the club.

Stryker comes off stage. He's sweaty and pumped. This has been a huge success—he can't believe how well he did tonight. *Where is Luna?* Stryker is ready to take her out to celebrate his standing ovations. He checks his phone and reads and rereads Luna's hostile text.

LUNA (TEXT)

I just had an interesting conversation with someone who says they know you. Jackson! Jackson Caine, ring a bell?!

Following his performance at The Fury, the next few days are a whirlwind of media attention. Stryker's video went viral in a matter of hours. It's a trifecta! His all-American good looks, plus being the son of a billionaire, combined with Quarantina, the perfect song to define the mood of the country. It's a story everyone wants to hear. He's all over the internet, in the usual places on YouTube, Facebook, and *Flikrz.* With Stryker's bloodline and talent, television outlets in the United States and Europe are featuring him on their infotainment programs. Just as the virus went global, as if he were the virus, Stryker Caine has gone ultra-viral.

Luna can't keep up with all the social media attention. She paces the floor of her meager apartment with her phone in hand. It's making her more and more angry realizing she helped perpetuate Stryker's image under false pretenses.

"I feel like a fool for ever knowing him," Luna says to Santana who she is simultaneously FaceTiming with. "Or actually, *not* knowing him."

Santana can't get a word in, so he just listens to Luna's ranting, nodding his head.

"Was he just playing with me the whole time? Was everything fake?" Luna says, sobbing into the phone.

She wishes she'd never met Stryker. The worst of it is she felt she was falling in love with him. Now here she is heartbroken.

Ever since his performance Stryker's cell phone is blowing up. His email box is exploding, and he has picked up thousands of new followers on all of his social networks.

There are even paparazzi hovering outside his apartment building. But all Stryker can think of is talking to Luna. She won't answer his calls. He's left forty-three messages begging her to at least listen to him. He didn't mean to hurt her. It's true he was living a double life, but he desperately needs to explain why.

STRYKER (TEXT)
Hey man.

LOGAN (TEXT)
Hey Stryker! I see you everywhere congratulations! I guess you are giving up your Fury shows?

STRYKER (TEXT)
Dunno exactly what I am doing yet. But I need a favor.

LOGAN (TEXT)
Sure thing, what is it?

STRYKER (TEXT)
Come over and I will tell you.

Logan, the drummer from Stryker's band, arrives at Stryker's apartment in forty minutes. Logan assumes Stryker wants to talk to him about the future of him continuing to play with him. Logan is all about it. Stryker has a huge following on social media now and is getting worldwide attention. Logan hopes it will rub off on him. He's tired of trying to make ends meet. Maybe he can even quit his day job.

Logan is surprised to see Stryker lives in such a crappy building, him being the son of Merritt Caine. He pushes past the paparazzi, rings the intercom, and after being buzzed in by Stryker, Logan makes his way up the five flights.

Once inside he sees Stryker is worn out, his eyes red, and he's wearing crumpled clothes.

"I need you to be me, divert the paparazzi, so I can go next door and see my girl, Luna," Stryker says, not mincing words.

"Oh-kaay?" Logan agrees, not really understanding how he'll pull that off. He has just walked through all the celebrity photographers huddled outside Stryker's apartment.

Stryker tells Logan to wear his western shirt from The Fury show and a baseball cap pulled way down over his eyes and of course a mask over his face. Logan's hair is brown, but he recently got a buzz cut and can hide his hair under the cap. Stryker gives him large black sunglasses to top off his disguise and tells him to just keep walking down the street east and hopefully lead the paparazzi away from his building. Stryker watches from the window, and when Logan is far enough away, he makes his escape to Luna's apartment.

Standing outside her building Stryker waits, trying to look inconspicuous. He needs to be buzzed in. After fifteen minutes he sees a delivery guy approaching, carrying a brown food delivery bag.

"Hey man, what apartment are you going to?" Stryker says, hoping he doesn't look menacing.

"14B."

"That's my girls place, give me the bag and I'll give you forty bucks for your trouble."

"No way."

Stryker stretches his hand out, showing him two twenty-dollar bills. After a minute, the delivery guy takes the money and hands over the bag. Stryker presses the button on Luna's mailbox and is buzzed inside.

Luna has not gone anywhere since the event and has been ordering food delivery for days. She had Chinese three nights in a row and tonight she's getting Thai. Hearing a knock on her door she peeks through the peep hole to see a man in a hat with a paper bag looking at the floor. She opens the door to what she thinks is the delivery man and sees Stryker's blue eyes in a mask looking at her. She tries to close the door on him, but Stryker holds it open with the palm of his hand.

"Wait Luna, just let me explain," Stryker implores as he steps inside.

Luna folds her arms over her chest. She knew this moment would eventually come so why not just get it over with.

"What?" Luna says angrily. "What can you possibly say?"

"That I'm sorry. I never meant to deceive you," Stryker says in the sincerest voice he can muster.

"Deceive me? You lied to me. For weeks!" Luna grabs the bag of food from him and walks behind the counter in her kitchenette.

"I…I couldn't tell you. I had finally gotten myself into a place where no one knew who I was related to."

"So what's the problem with being one of the richest kids in America?"

Luna doesn't feel even a little bit sorry for him. She

feels sorry for herself for having ever gotten involved with Stryker. "Now, please leave," Luna says, taking the food containers out of the bag. "I want to eat my dinner."

Stryker ignores her, sits down on her couch. "I wanted to make it on my own, not because of my father," Stryker says, putting his head in his hands, hoping Luna will come over and console him.

"Well you didn't even make it on your own. I promoted you. Then you made a complete fool of me," Luna says, glaring at him.

Stryker is surprised. What is Luna even talking about? He was playing the songs. In his mind Luna had little to do with his success.

"Luna, I got discovered because of my talent, it was only a matter of time," Stryker says, raising his voice.

Luna wants to throw the food at him. *Oh my God, what a narcissist! He needs to get over himself!*

"I filled the room with all those social media "A" listers!" Luna shouts at him.

Stryker stands up. He can't believe this.

"Exactly. You told me *you* were the influencer!" Stryker says. "But in reality, you are not an influencer, you were relying on them!"

Right after Stryker says this, he knows he's gone too far.

Luna bursts into tears. *How can he be so cruel.* "Get out! Get the fuck out of my house!"

Enraged, Luna steps out from behind the kitchen counter. She gets right in Stryker's face—her cheeks wet with tears. They stand there for a moment staring at each other, both seeing red. Stryker knows his attempt at apologizing has failed miserably, now it's worse than ever.

"Luna…I am sorry. I didn't mean it," Stryker says, trying to calm her down.

"I said get out!" Luna screams at him, opening her apartment door.

Stryker walks out of Luna's apartment and as the door slams shuts, he hears her put the final nail in his coffin.

"I wish I never met you on the roof that day!"

CHAPTER 7

STRYKER (TEXT)

Hey

LOGAN (TEXT)

How did it go?

STRYKER (TEXT)

Not well. Things went really badly.

LOGAN (TEXT)

Sorry man

STRYKER (TEXT)

What happened with the paparazzi?

LOGAN (TEXT)

They followed me for a couple blocks but then they realized it wasn't you.

STRYKER (TEXT)

Where are you now?

LOGAN (TEXT)

At Mongoose versus Cobra, come down and drown your sorrows

STRYKER (TEXT)

Yeah see you in a few.

When Stryker arrives at Mongoose versus Cobra, he spots Logan sitting at the far end of the bar.

"What are we drinking?" Stryker says, slumping into the seat beside him.

"Tequila. My friend, we are doing Tequila shots."

Stryker sees Logan is glassy eyed with several empty shot glasses in front of him.

"It was cool being famous. Even though it was fake fame, being hounded by a group of photographers really boosts a guy's self-esteem," Logan says, laughing.

Stryker doesn't say anything. He wants to get drunk and numb quickly. He holds two fingers up, signaling to the bartender to send over two more shots.

"I really screwed up this time Logan, I should have been honest right from the beginning..." Stryker laments, throwing back the Tequila shot.

"I had no idea it was so serious," Logan says. "I thought it was just a fling."

"It was the real thing," Stryker says. "She was the one."

"Look, maybe it's not actually over, you know how women are, maybe there's still a chance... I wouldn't give up just yet."

"No. There's no getting over this one, I shouldn't have been so secretive. I should have trusted her more and told her who I really was," Stryker says, slamming his fist on the bar.

"Yeah, you could have let us all in on that secret. You know I always had your back, and apparently so did Luna."

"Sorry man, I guess I still have a lot to learn about friendship."

"Aaron and Trent are on route. We all want to know what you plan to do with the band. Now that you've been '*discovered.*'"

"I really haven't thought about it yet."

Stryker is only thinking about Luna. *Now the last memory I will have of her is how incredibly betrayed she felt.* He feels there's no coming back from that. She's so angry. Trying to make himself feel better, Stryker opens the hologram juke box app on his phone and selects the vintage song "Games People Play." The lyrics by Joe South are eerily identifiable. A three-dimensional image of the 60s musician in a polyester double-breasted suit appears beside Stryker. Logan and Stryker watch the performance as if the music legend is there in the bar. The twang of Joe South playing the sitar is as haunting as the black and white beam of light projecting the musician singing and swaying to the music.

Aaron and Trent walk in, bringing with them three extremely attractive women. Two are blonde and look Scandinavian. The other is Asian with long black hair. They all look like supermodels.

"Ladies, as you requested, I present to you the infamous Stryker Caine," Trent says loudly.

Stryker cringes as the women surround him, touching his shoulders and chest as if they know him well.

"Relax. man, relax. I promise they won't hurt you," Trent says in amusement.

Aaron motions the bartender over and orders Tequila shots for everyone. Yes, more alcohol, Stryker thinks. I need more alcohol. He downs his fourth and then fifth Tequila shot, hoping the effects will set in soon. *Maybe this is all just a bad dream.* The two blonde women, seeing they are being rejected, turn their flirtations toward Trent. The Asian woman is much more intent on capturing Stryker's attention and is not giving up. She squeezes herself in between Stryker and Logan, trying to get even closer to him. Stryker barely notices her presence as he stares down at the next three shots lined up in front of him.

"Hey, are you going to join the rest of us or is this a party of one?" she says jokingly.

Stryker looks up at her as if she's speaking a foreign language. "Sorry. It's been a really bad day, I'm not very good company right now." He tilts his head back, swallowing the three shots in succession.

"Do you want to talk about it?" she says, seductively touching his hand. "Because I'm a great listener."

Stryker is starting to feel the sensation of the alcohol building in his veins. Trent puts two more shots in front of him, and Stryker quickly drinks them down.

"I'm Jade. Like the jewel."

"My girlfriend's name was Luna, like the moon."

"Oh, what happened to her?" Jade asks.

"She dumped me," Stryker confesses.

"Her loss," Jade says, stroking his thigh in one long hard motion.

Another round of Tequila shots arrive. Stryker takes one in each hand and gulps them down. "My loss," he says. "She was the love of my life. I know that now."

Stryker has not ever had such intense feelings for any woman and now he has lost her, for what he is sure will be forever.

"She was so beautiful…" he continues "…and sweet and kind." He hates talking about Luna in the past tense.

Jade rolls her eyes and pushes her shot over to him. "You need this more than I do," she says.

Stryker drinks the shot without thanking her. He can feel himself losing his balance on the stool.

Jade props him up with her shoulder. "Don't worry, I will take good care of you," she whispers in his ear.

Stryker feels himself slowly losing consciousness. He doesn't care. He's in sheer misery.

When Stryker wakes up, he realizes it's morning and he must have blacked out. He's lying on his back, looking at the ceiling. He feels disoriented and his head is pounding. He's naked and the white bed sheets are twisted around his legs. He looks around the room and wonders where he is. Then he sees her. It's Jade from the bar, and she's lying on her stomach beside him, her long black hair strewn across her naked back.

Oh shit! He can't remember how he got here or if he had sex with the woman beside him. He does know he needs to get out, fast! He carefully and quietly rolls himself out of the bed, not wanting to wake her up. Once standing, he gathers his clothes, which are in various locations across the floor, and gets dressed in a panic. He takes one last look at Jade to make sure she's still sleeping, then he makes his escape, not looking back.

❧

It's a day after Luna's breakup with Stryker and she's miserable. She keeps going over and over what happened in her mind. The way they met. The way he smiled at her. The way he smelled. The way he would hold her all through the night. *What a complete waste of my time!* Now here she is, unemployed, without health insurance, without a man. She's depressed. She doesn't have any energy to do anything. It's 1:00 p.m. and she's still in bed when Santana FaceTimes her. Luna almost doesn't answer it. She's in no mood to speak to anyone, not even her best friend.

"Hi Santana, I'm taking a nap," she says, yawning.

"I wouldn't think you could sleep after all of this. I mean, the latest is sickening," Santana says cautiously, not sure Luna has seen it yet on social media, and he wants to tread lightly.

"What did he finally do, an interview? He's so full of himself, what did he say?" Luna says lethargically.

She can barely keep her eyes open—has been crying on and off for the past twenty-four hours. She didn't wanted to break down in front of Stryker. She wishes he had not seen her cry. Luna did not want Stryker to know just how much he hurt her.

Santana doesn't say anything, he just looks at her through the phone.

Startled, Luna sits up in bed, sitting cross legged, holding the cell phone up above her, away from her face. "What Santana? What did he say? Did he say something about me?" Luna is both excited and curious.

Had Stryker publicly asked for her forgiveness? That's what he should do, he fucked up so bad! Luna imagines Stryker seated at a table giving a press conference. Camera's flashing at him while he begs for her forgiveness, professing his love for her. They had not yet said the *love* word to each other. But they were on the cusp of it. Now would be the perfect time, Luna thinks.

"If he apologizes to me in front of the world…maybe, just maybe I'll give him another chance," Luna tells Santana.

She's now seriously considering it. *A public apology from one of the richest men in America would spread like mad on social media.* Luna could save face. Not only would Darcy find out who her boyfriend is, and that he's rich and famous, she would know it's due in part to Luna successfully promoting him. Luna relishes in the thought of her name being blasted alongside Stryker Caine! She will let him come crawling back to her because she does love him so much it hurts.

Santana interrupts her thoughts. "Boo, it's bad…it's all over the internet," Santana says. "Check TMZ."

Luna is scared. *Has Stryker been in an accident? Is he in the hospital?* Luna puts the phone down on her pillow and grabs her iPad from the nightstand. She goes to TMZ's website. The home page loads quickly onto the screen, and then Luna's mouth drops open.

The headline reads—"Jackson Stryker Caine's sexcapade with international model in New York City apartment!"

Beneath the headline is a photograph of a stunning Asian model lying on top of Stryker's bare chest. They are against a mass of white pillows in a bed. The photo is a selfie taken by the naked woman who smiles into the camera. Stryker's eyes are closed, and his golden hair is a mess. The woman is pinching Stryker's right nipple. The caption beneath the photo reads, "My night of ecstasy with Stryker Caine!"

Luna snaps closed the lid of her iPad's case. Devastated, she feels herself becoming physically ill, then she wails, "How could he? We just broke up!"

"Luna? Luna!" Santana yells from her phone. "Pick up, pick up!"

Santana wishes he had told her in person so he could hug and calm her. Dammit, he thinks in hindsight, what have I done? He continues to call out Luna's name through the phone. It feels like an eternity passes before she finally picks up her cell phone and speaks.

"What an asshole! How humiliating!" Luna cries.

Santana can't think of anything to say and stays silent.

"I have to go," Luna says, clicking off the call. She feels like smashing everything in her apartment. She throws her cell phone against the wall directly in front of her, just missing the TV. She throws it so hard it splits open and falls in pieces onto the hardwood floor.

"Fuck!" she screams.

Lying back down, Luna pulls the covers over her head and sobs.

CHAPTER 8

STRYKER AND HIS band have been touring around the country for months. Before he left he called Luna, but her number was disconnected. Considering everything that has happened, Stryker knows he has no chance of fixing things.

He moves to the west coast. He writes a song called "Luna." It quickly goes up the charts, but he doesn't hear from her. Stryker Caine is a bona fide rock star! All his shows are sold out in minutes. He hates that Trent is constantly bringing groupies around after each show. He's not interested and is amazed how they will do any sex act Trent demands. He feels lost. All he can do is concentrate on making music.

Logan tries to drag him out to parties in Malibu, but Stryker always refuses. He likes living on the ocean, listening to the continuous sound of the waves. He sits on his deck composing songs. Like clockwork, every other day a press drone circles him overhead. He gives it the finger and retreats into his house.

It's Saturday night, and Stryker is fixing himself another drink when Logan FaceTimes him.

"Hey man, come out tonight. There's a party you can't miss in Carbon Beach," Logan says.

"Not into it, bro," Stryker says passively.

"It's been months, have some fun. You have become a recluse and it's weirding me out. How long are your fingernails now?"

"What?" Stryker asks, not understanding.

"Clean yourself up. Shave, cut your hair, file your nails. Become a human again. You don't need to keep feeling sorry for yourself," Logan needles him.

"I'll think about it," Stryker says, clicking off the call.

Stryker gives in and takes a self-driving limousine to Carbon Beach, to a party thrown by a well-known celebrity. It's a white party. Stryker has obliged and is wearing white trousers, a white t-shirt, and white sneakers.

He quickly adapts to being famous again. Being the son of Merritt Caine, Stryker has experienced the mass media since he was a small child. Because he's an only child, the media has always had an intense interest in whatever he did. Now that Stryker is also a successful pop star, he's a double target. He no longer hides from the paparazzi, he knows it's useless. The machine fire of camera flashes follow him wherever he goes. Ever since he lost Luna, Stryker feels he deserves the lack of privacy. He plays the part of a victim very well.

The party is held in a white mansion located on the beach. The residence is a modern palace made almost entirely of glass windows. Stryker, resentful and combative, makes his way through the bevy of anxious photographers positioned in front of the enormous estate. He scrambles up the wide stone steps until he is safely inside. In the foyer he walks through the antimicrobial chemical mist device into the main great room.

Stryker's presence at the party does not go unnoticed. Men and women turn to look at him with giant eyes when he walks by. He's forgotten how incredibly handsome he is. He has settled into feeling sorry for himself most days. Tonight is no different, his mood is self-loathing, he just wants a scotch and to find Logan.

Stryker drifts over to the multitude of buffet tables—there is a caviar station, a sushi station, a seafood station, a sirloin station, a pasta station, and finally a dessert station. He samples the sushi station. As he is stuffing a mahi mahi roll into his mouth, he notices a tall brunette standing beside the table.

"Beautiful setup," he exclaims. "You did a bang-up job."

The woman looks at him, pausing before saying, "Well, thank you."

Stryker is so weary of the famous pompous people he sees at these parties. He's happy to talk with someone down to earth like the caterer.

"What's your favorite?" she asks.

Stryker looks at the buffet tables then at the woman. He has not observed how lovely she is until now. She's tall, wearing all black, and has dimples on each cheek.

"I like the sushi mostly and the dessert," Stryker says, wiping his mouth.

"Good to know," the woman says, picking up a sushi roll and popping it into her mouth.

Stryker laughs. He likes how bold the woman is. He's

not seen a caterer eat their own food so openly at an event. "Careful," he says, "the hostess may be watching."

"Oh, I hear she is a real gem," the woman says.

"You never really know though," Stryker says.

He likes this woman's style. She's easy going and warm. He knows he needs no introduction, but he feels compelled to do so, so he can find out the name of this mysterious woman.

"I'm Stryker," he says. "Stryker Caine."

"I know who you are," she says, smiling.

She has a provocative smile and her teeth are perfect. Stryker waits a moment, but the woman is not offering up her name.

"And you are?" he asks, extending his hand.

"I'm Charlotte," she says, "Charlotte Belle…and this is my house."

Charlotte Belle is a well-known Hollywood actress. She's starred in films alongside all the major movie stars. Stryker sucks in his breath. *Of course she is, that's why she looks so familiar.* He's embarrassed he's mistaken her for the caterer.

"My apologies, I didn't recognize you," Stryker says.

"I just did something new with my hair, so that must be why," Charlotte says, winking at him.

"Yes, that must be it," Stryker says, flirting back at her.

Stryker likes her sense of humor. Rarely does he meet anyone in these party circles willing to laugh at themselves. Stryker wonders why she's wearing all black at a white party but says nothing. It must be because she's the host, he thinks.

"I truly am having a good time," Stryker continues. "Your house is a masterpiece."

"Thank you. Now come join me on the observation deck," Charlotte says, looping her arm under his. "That's where the VIPs are, where you belong."

Charlotte leads him down a corridor. At the end is a circular metal staircase that rises up to what must be twenty-five feet high. They start climbing. Charlotte goes first and is three steps ahead of him. Stryker watches her firm buttocks go up and down as she takes each step. He can't believe he's with Charlotte Belle. As she climbs, she occasionally turns her head to look down and smile at Stryker. There must be 100 steps, Stryker thinks. He's almost out of breath when he reaches the landing. The floor is made of glass and he sees beneath him the entire stairwell coiling upward.

"Maybe we should have taken the elevator," Charlotte ponders, looking at Stryker. "But it's so much prettier this way..."

Trying to conceal he's winded, Stryker simply says, "Indeed, it is."

Charlotte slips underneath a billowing transparent white curtain. When Stryker follows, he finds himself standing on the rooftop. In front of him is the ocean. The water stretches across the landscape for miles. Stryker listens to the slow rumbling sound of waves rolling out to sea, the momentary pause, and then the roaring crash of the white waves breaking onto the sand. The endless motion of the sea before him is hypnotic and peaceful.

Charlotte stands beside him, saying nothing. Her brown hair blows in a halo around her beautiful face. He's about to speak when they're interrupted by a booming male voice behind them.

"Stryker Caine."

Stryker turns around and recognizes Nikola Maltese. The heartthrob actor from numerous American and European films.

At the sight of the movie idol, Stryker quickly snaps himself out of the moment he's just experienced with Charlotte.

"Great to meet you. I'm Nick. I love that song, "Quarantina," Nikola says, holding out his hand.

Stryker grasps it, and Nikola gives him a vigorous handshake hello. Stryker remembers seeing posts on social media linking Charlotte Belle and Nikola Maltese as a hot Hollywood couple. Their relationship status was constantly in flux, no one could ever keep track of their on and off romance. Stryker wonders what phase they're in at this point. They seem cordial enough, but Nikola isn't touching her enough to imply he's with her.

"I like your latest song called 'Luna,'" Charlotte says. "I absolutely love the lyrics…"

Charlotte softly sings the first verse.

> *"If I find my way back to you—I'll show the world they never knew*
>
> *All of me just for you, it's all I could ever do"*

"You really must have broken her heart," Charlotte exclaims.

"Come on, let's get back to the others," Nikola says to Charlotte.

"Again, nice meeting you," Nikola says to Stryker in a

dismissive tone then turns and walks away with Charlotte not far behind him.

They are almost back to the small crowd gathered on the rooftop when Charlotte stops and runs back to Stryker. "Quick, give me your phone," she says.

Stryker hands her his phone.

"Unlock it," Charlotte says, handing it back to him.

Stryker unlocks his phone and gives it back to her. He likes how the imprint of her dimples shows whenever she speaks. She is typing into his phone at a frenzied pace. "I put in my number. If you're ever in the neighborhood, give me a call."

Stryker takes his phone from her and watches her hurry away to catch up with Nikola who has almost reached the group of VIPs.

Stryker finds his way out of the house and goes home. He searches for Charlotte Belle's name on his television and finds two of her old movies. He begins watching her in *Who Comes Knocking* and falls asleep on his sofa.

He has vivid dreams of Charlotte. He's about to kiss her lips when she suddenly changes into Luna. Stryker is overcome with elation, seeing her light brown skin and full lips before him. He feels whole again as he caresses her body but wakes up with a shudder, realizing he's still on the couch and it was all just a dream. As he makes his way into his bedroom he realizes he's not over Luna. He wonders if he ever will be. He lies down on his side in a fetal position and tries to fall back asleep.

Chapter 9

LUNA'S CAREER HAS taken off, she is now a true influencer. From her initial association publicizing Stryker Caine, Luna has amassed over a million followers. She's promoting designer clothing, eco-friendly food, natural skincare, and even vitamin supplements. Luna receives a commission on all sales and is paid $50,000 per post. She's an ambassador in hot demand. With her increasing success, Luna's confidence grows. She's no longer the shy introvert hiding her beauty. Luna is the person she has always wanted to be, and she knows her opinion is golden.

She still thinks about Stryker. As much as she fights it, he occupies a space in her heart. Luna even moves to California to escape any memories of him. She flies Santana out to the west coast so he can escort her to the many award shows and after parties. Luna was sure she'd cross paths with Stryker at one of these elite events, but she never does. Eventually Luna tried to compartmentalize any memory of him. She becomes a workaholic focused on growing her following on social media.

It's Wednesday morning and Luna is checking her many DMs when one message in particular catches her eye.

Luna this is Penelope, I am Simon Caswell's assistant. Mr. Caswell is seeking to hire you to represent him on social media and rehab his bad boy image.

Simon Caswell is a wealthy, powerful person in the pharmaceuticals industry. He has hundreds of patents and ranks among the greatest inventors on the Forbes 100 List. Luna is curious, but she knows Simon Caswell has a reputation as being an exceedingly difficult person to work with. So she ignores the message.

Luna checks her other social accounts and her email. She finds on every platform she has received a message from Penelope seeking to hire her to improve Simon Caswell's image.

What a pest! If he's going to be this persistent, I can only imagine what type of annoying client he would be. She needs to put a stop to this before it goes any further so messages Penelope back.

Hello Penelope, thank you for contacting me, however I am booked with all the clients I can handle at this time. If something changes, I will contact you. ~ Luna

Moments after she hits send, her cell phone rings. The caller ID warns it's an "Unknown Caller." Nonetheless Luna answers it on the 3rd ring.

"Hello?" Luna says.

"Hello Luna, this is Penelope, Simon Caswell's assistant." The woman's voice sounds young and wavering.

"Yes, I just replied to your message. I'm not available to pick up any new clients," Luna says firmly.

"What would it take for you to become available? Mr. Caswell is prepared to pay as much as you need to represent him."

Luna is silent, busy Googling him on her tablet, expecting to see he has recently committed a crime. Each article she scrolls through mentions that Simon Caswell is a genius, but he's also a loose cannon. His latest project is developing a vaccine that would morph naturally to address any mutation in the virus.

"Hello? Hello? Miss James?" Penelope says nervously.

"Yes, I am here. I am sorry, I just haven't the time," Luna says.

She's not budging. Luna has read about the barbarity Simon Caswell inflicts upon his employees. How he even makes male colleagues cry. Luna does not want any part of it.

"Penelope, sorry. I'm just swamped. Also, I don't think I'm the right fit for the position," Luna says in an apologetic tone.

"Right fit? Mr. Caswell assures you, you are the right person for the job. The press doesn't treat him fairly. Simon Caswell truly is one of the nicest human beings I know," Penelope pleads.

Luna is suspicious. How would Simon Caswell know she's the person for the job? They have not even met.

"Mr. Caswell will pay $200,000 per post and provide you with an unlimited expense account," Penelope says forcefully.

This gets Luna's attention. Wow, $200,000 per post is four times as much as she's charging.

"I don't know if it's even doable. Cleaning up his image could take my posting several times per day..." Luna counters.

"That is acceptable. Mr. Caswell is fine with you posting all throughout the day."

Luna is astonished. Penelope is starting to wear her down.

How bad could it possibly be, for that kind of money? Having the influential Simon Caswell as a client...even if for a little while, it would make me even richer and practically guarantee attracting more elite clientele! Plus, I need something like this to show everyone I have arrived!

Luna has almost convinced herself to accept the offer when she hears a cha-ching ding go off on her cell phone.

"One moment," Luna says, putting the call on hold.

She scrolls through her phone, looking over her apps. She sees she has a message on Venmo. She opens the payment app and sees she has a received a deposit of $125,000 into her account from Simon Caswell. The message reads—

Luna, I look forward to a winning partnership - Warm regards, Simon

Oh my God, this guy's incredible! She hasn't even agreed to accept the position and he's already sending her money. Luna returns to her call with Penelope.

"If he agrees to $250,000 per post with an unlimited expense account, I will take the time to consider it," Luna says stoically in hopes this will be enough to get rid of Simon Caswell, anticipating he will be deeply offended by her reluctance to barely entertain the lucrative opportunity.

"Done!" Penelope says with a smile in her voice. "I will

have a messenger drop off the contract as soon as possible for your consideration. What is your address please?"

Luna gives Penelope her address and says goodbye. As soon as the call is finished, her hands begin shaking. She can't believe what has just happened. Luna immediately calls Santana on the East Coast.

"Santana! I have news…"

Santana is drinking a protein shake, listening to Luna rant about Simon Caswell. He's heard all about Simon Caswell and his sleezy antics on the internet.

"Santana, this guy is said to be a supreme asshole. His ego is so big, he Venmoed me $125,000 before I even said yes. I still haven't said yes," Luna squeals into the phone.

"It's worth doing for the money…" Santana says.

"And it will lead to bigger things," Luna says, finishing his sentence.

"Exactly! You deserve this and all your success so far."

"Thanks Boo, you are always there for me. How are you doing?"

"The same. It's so cold out and the virus is in full force here in Manhattan," Santana says, looking out his window. He sees pedestrians in heavy coats with masks on going about their daily business. Feeling protective of his best friend he urges her to be cautious. "Be careful of this one."

"Of course. Don't worry even a little bit. I'm a big girl," Luna says reassuringly.

"Well I guess Mama will be buying a new pair of shoes," Santana says.

"...and a matching bag," Luna enthuses.

"And a matching hat," they say at the same time and both laugh.

"I love you, Santana."

"I love you too. Now go do great things. I will be watching."

Luna smiles and clicks off the call.

Simon Caswell Offends Again! was the headline on the *L.A. Times* home page. Simon Caswell is skimming through Google News. He's meeting Luna James in a matter of minutes and wants to be prepared with a story, should she ask him about any damaging articles. Every article mentions he's a germophobe. *Damn right.* He feels his extreme fear of germs and obsession with cleanliness is an asset in the current COVID-25 environment. He takes pride in having a germ-free workplace. The walls, office furniture, and air are sprayed with an industrial strength bacterial ridding agent every six hours. It's evident Simon's efforts to produce a vaccine for the virus is mostly a personal goal. He hopes a cure will help alleviate his severe OCD.

Simon is tall and has the thick body of a weightlifter. He has a full head of wavy brown hair and dark brown eyes and is considered handsome by all accounts. He's in his late thirties, vain, and detests getting older. He's from a middle-class family and because of his size was known as a bully in high school and college. Not much has changed since then—Simon enjoys pushing people around and getting his way. This means he's both hated and feared in the business world. He doesn't see this as a problem, he actually enjoys it.

His enormous office is in the tallest office building in Los Angeles and has the word Caswell in gold letters on the buildings' top floor. Penelope announces through the intercom, "Luna James has arrived."

"Send her in," Simon says. He stands up and buttons the jacket of his classic navy pinstriped suit. He applies some hand sanitizer and is walking around his massive desk just as Luna comes through the double doors of his office.

"Hello, Luna," he says calmly, pretending not to be phased by her incredible beauty. Luna is wearing a white silk tank top, a black pencil skirt, and black high heels. She carries a gray laptop bag. Simon thinks to himself, She is luscious. Oh, the things I am going to do to her. He already has his end game planned. It's true she made it difficult in the beginning, Simon remembers. Days ago, he was screaming at Penelope, asking what was taking so long. Why would Luna not agree to sign the contract? Who did Luna think she was anyway? That's behind him now. Luna has signed the contract. As far as he's concerned, she is bought. Another done deal.

"Hello, Simon." Luna smells a whiff of his cologne and scrunches up her nose. *Oh blech, he even smells bad.* Think of the money Luna, think of where this will take you, she keeps saying to herself. Simon has not asked her to take a seat, so Luna stands uncomfortably as he looks her up and down.

"So, I hear you are very good at what you do," Simon says in a condescending tone.

Luna opens her mouth to reply but quickly realizes he's just getting started.

"I am very good at what I do also," Simon brags, "by evidence of my mass fortune and empire. But for whatever reason people seem to get the wrong impression of me, so I just need you to smooth it out a little...make me more of a humanist."

Simon walks over to one of the large windows in his office, and staring off into the horizon, goes on with his monologue.

"You know, like all the work I do for the kids, the homeless—I give a lot of money to the less fortunate..."

Simon has his back to her, which Luna thinks is rude. Her feet hurt standing there. She shifts her weight to her heels. H*ow long is he going to drone on?* She's questioning her decision to take on Simon as a client when he swiftly turns around and says, "But it's almost the end of the day. What we should do is go talk about this on my yacht... over dinner."

"No. I don't feel comfortable with that," Luna says immediately.

"Ah well... I was thinking at least go on my yacht and we have...ah...better scenery to discuss how we should approach this." Simon is not accepting her rejection.

"On your boat? Anyway, how are we even going to get there. We are in the middle of L.A., and it's the middle of rush hour."

"That's not a problem," Simon says as he applies more hand sanitizer.

He grins at Luna. To avoid touching the buttons he

presses the intercom button with a pen and says, “Is the chopper ready?”

Chopper? Oh no… She grows tired, knowing yet another guy wants to impress her. *Chopper? Who even says that? What is this, 1980?*

“I don’t know if that’s such a good idea,” Luna says. “I have other…”

“Oh, I insist, and besides the sea air is cleaner,” Simon interrupts her.

Luna knows Simon has a point. The air on his yacht would be COVID free.

“All right,” Luna says, wishing she’d worn sandals.

“On board there are disposal flip flops you can wear,” Simon says, almost reading her mind.

It’s Luna’s first time in a volocopter and the experience is exhilarating. She’s glad she’s not expected to make small talk over the humming of the propellers. She can feel Simon looking at her. The volocopter makes a sharp upright turn, and she has no choice but to brace herself on Simon’s arm. Without looking at him, she mumbles, “Excuse me.”

Simon smiles. He had the route programmed to make that turn whenever he brings a beautiful woman on his volocopter. The volocopter lands safely on his forty-foot yacht. Luna has removed her heels and is barefoot on the deck. Her long curly black hair blows in an uproar around her face. She follows Simon to the front of the vessel and sees a round table covered with a white tablecloth. There’s a red rose in a vase, lit candles, and an ice bucket with a bottle of champagne in the center of the table. Luna feels she is on a date from the television show *The Bachelor*—the scene is so cliché.

With a small huff, she shakes her head and frowns. What else can she do? She's trapped on a yacht until Simon Caswell decides it's time to go back to Los Angeles. *It looks like a date, it feels like a date...it is a date.* She sits down across from Simon.

"It's a beautiful sunset, don't you think?" Simon says, peering at her.

Simon is overtly looking at her breasts, and he licks his lips and gazes at her sinewy body. He imagines her naked below deck doing whatever he wants. A deckhand appears and as if on cue opens the bottle of champagne and pours each of them a glass. Luna ignores Simon's comment and tries to change the subject back to business.

"So, the first thing we need to do is demonstrate your humanitarian efforts," she says.

"That's perfect. We already have a charity auction lined up," Simon says, pretending to be interested. "And on the 12th, I'm receiving a humanitarian award from ISMC for alleviating the less fortunate among us."

He barely listens to what Luna says. He's fixated on undressing her.

"Oh, and I'm going to Paris next week. You must accompany me," he says as an afterthought.

Luna takes an involuntary step back. *Must? I must accompany him? Who does this guy think he is?*

"That won't be necessary. Everything we need to work

on can be done virtually," Luna says, politely maintaining her composure.

"Per our contract, you are obligated to be by my side at all of my business events," Simon says, leaning forward across the small table.

Luna leans back. This must have been hidden in the many paragraphs she neglected to read in her contract. *I should have had a lawyer look it over. Why did I give in to Penelope's pressure?* Luna hopes Simon is bluffing, and she stalls for time.

"I will need to consult my lawyer on that," Luna says tactfully.

"Of course. I'm sure it's in there." He loves seeing Luna squirm with anxiety. "Now let's enjoy our dinner," he says, sliding his fork into his steak.

Luna has lost her appetite. She wonders how she let this happen. She wants to cry but doesn't want to give Simon the satisfaction of seeing her in tears.

"Yes, let's," she says, smiling. *I can outsmart you, you bastard! Just you wait and see.*

The Charity Auction Simon Caswell is to attend is held in New York City. Luna is excited to be back in Manhattan—she's making money and able to hang out with Santana.

Luna has forgotten how bad the virus is in the Big Apple. It's remained the epicenter, and it's almost in the same state as when she moved out to California. The city feels hollow and exhausted. The streets remain on the empty side, with a minimal amount of masked people walking on the sidewalks.

She's staying at Santana's apartment, so she can spend as much time with him as possible. Santana is always cheerful, and it rubs off on Luna's mood. She's getting ready to head downtown to meet Simon and wants Santana's advice on how best to handle him.

"Don't ever let him see how you feel," Santana advises. "Keeping a poker face will drive him crazy."

Luna nods. She has a bunch of black bobby pins between her lips and is trying to figure out how to wear her cascade of black curls.

"Remember the goal is to get under his skin, not the other way around," Santana lectures. Then carefully he pries, "Have you heard from Stryker?"

"Santana, you ask me that every time you see me. The answer is still no." Exasperated, Luna takes the bobby pins out of her mouth. She turns away from the mirror and scowls at him.

"Maybe you should contact him? You are so successful now in your own right."

Santana is half right. I am now one of the most well-known influencers on both coasts.

"I will never contact him. I wouldn't give him the satisfaction," Luna says, clearly bothered. She knows Santana means no harm, that it comes from his caring about her, but just hearing Stryker's name still hits her like a ton of bricks.

"Girl, you are too stubborn for your own good sometimes," Santana mumbles, regretting he has said anything about Stryker. He sees Luna's on edge and wants to hug her in support, but no one does that anymore, not in the age of the virus. No more giving Italian kisses on each cheek either. Not even air kisses.

"Luna, I'm sorry. And you are beautiful," he says instead, hoping she'll stop fussing with her hair and forget he meddled. She has become more confident over the past several months, and he likes the new Luna. Now when she walks into a room and all eyes are on her, she expects it. She demands the attention. She is Luna James and she wants everyone to know it.

"Yes, I am," Luna says to her reflection. "I *am* beautiful."

Simon Caswell likes all the attention he gets walking with Luna through the silent auction. She looks amazing, he thinks, knowing photos of them will be on *Flikrz* instantly. Luna doesn't notice the attention—she can smell the wealth in the room. She looks at the items up for auction, these are not the everyday gift baskets. They are auctioning priceless experiences—a private cooking class with a famous chef at Le Cordon Bleu in London, a hands-on sailing excursion on the America's Cup yacht.

Luna keeps noticing a woman in a designer mask everywhere she walks with Simon. When they stop for a moment for glasses of wine, she sees the woman with mousy brown hair again, standing a few feet away. Luna is positive the masked woman is following them as she moves about the room with Simon. Because the woman is impeccably dressed Luna knows she's not a member of the media and the woman is not pretty enough to be an ex of Simon's.

Luna is fed up and intentionally stops walking abruptly so the woman bumps into her.

"Luuuna?" the woman says in a shrill voice. "Is that you?"

Luna would know that whiny voice anywhere. It's Darcy Brooks, her arch enemy from *Fashiondemic*.

"Oh, hi Darcy," Luna says, feigning a smile under her mask.

"Oh my God, it's so good to see you!" Darcy stutters. "I've seen your blog mentioned everywhere."

"Yeah, I can see you are literally following me," Luna says.

Darcy blushes with embarrassment.

"So, what are you up to Darcy, are you still with *Fashiondemic*?"

"No, no. *Fashiondemic* folded soon after you left, so I lost my job"

Luna already knows *Fashiondemic* is "On Hiatus," she just wanted to hear it come out of Darcy's mouth. Luna looks down her nose at Darcy and says, "Oh, so sorry to hear that. Simon and I are here bidding on items."

Luna slides her hand around his arm and hugs his bicep. "Isn't that right, Simon?"

"Yes darling," Simon says, playing along. "I'm just about to buy you that All-Access Pass to Stryker Caine's upcoming concert!"

"Oh, I love him!" Darcy cooes. "So nice to meet you Simon." Darcy holds her hand out to Simon in greeting.

Simon, a germaphobe and a snob, just looks at her.

"Well thank you, honey," Luna says, looking up at Simon. "Thank you very much."

"Weren't you dating him, Luna?" Darcy asks, completely confused.

"Oh, I'm with Simon now," Luna declares.

Simon turns to Luna, pulls down her mask, and kisses her full on the mouth. A flurry of clicks from cameras can be heard nearby. People have their cell phones out, filming the interaction.

Darcy watches in disbelief.

Simon and Luna have become a spectacle. Luna is repulsed by his kiss but doesn't let it show.

"Have to be going now, Darcy," Luna says, yanking Simon's arm.

"Oh, of course," Darcy replies, watching the two walk to the exit.

Simon is pleased with himself. He has kissed Luna when she least expected it. Sitting next to him in his black self-driving limousine, Luna fumes. Neither of them say a word as the black car whisks through the deserted New York City streets. Finally, Luna brakes the silence.

"That kiss was not necessary," she says, arms crossed against her chest.

"I wanted to convince your friend we were an item, wasn't that the game we were playing?" Simon says. He finds her pouting so amusing he's on the verge of laughing.

"Now that encounter will be all over social. I am here

to do a job! And that job is to clean up your image, not to damage it even further," Luna says harshly.

"Settle down, settle down," Simon says as if he's talking to a child.

This infuriates Luna even more. *He is so patronizing!* Then Luna remembers what Santana told her. *"Don't let him see he has gotten under your skin."* I must keep my composure, Luna thinks.

Looking out the car's window she sees they are headed down Park Avenue. "This isn't the way to Santana's apartment," Luna says, shooting a deadly look at Simon.

"We're going to my hotel for a nightcap," Simon says, his thin pale lips curled up into a closed mouth smile.

He places his hand on Luna's knee and moves it up her thigh. Luna firmly pushes his hand off her leg. She scoots forward and says into the car's voice activated GPS system, "Take me to 129 Highland Avenue in Queens."

Sitting back into the car seat she calmly looks at Simon. "I'm sorry if I gave you the wrong idea, but physical contact is not part of our agreement."

Simon blinks. Looking at Luna's face, he sees she's serious. Clearly this is not the night he will have Luna. *I will have her, just not tonight.* He squirts a glob of hand sanitizer into his palms and vigorously rubs his hands together then immerses himself into his cell phone, ignoring Luna the rest of the way to Santana's apartment.

CHAPTER 10

STRYKER IS DISAPPOINTED when he sees the photos of Luna with Simon Caswell on social media. He can't understand why Luna would be with that type of man. Simon Caswell is known as a pompous asshole everywhere online.

Stryker's last hit was "Luna," and for weeks he's been trying to write new music. But he can't come up with anything—he's so uninspired. He is picking at his guitar and humming when his cell phone rings. It's Jeremy, his agent.

"What's going on Jeremy?" Stryker asks, putting his cell phone on hands free mode.

"How's that new song coming?"

"It's not," Stryker says honestly.

"Well fear not, I have good news for you..."

"Lay it on me, I like good news," Stryker says.

"You have been chosen to be in a film...and not just any film...Chase Beckett's new movie."

Stryker is genuinely surprised Chase Beckett even knows who he is. "Chosen?"

"It's a small part," Jeremy continues, "but it's great exposure..."

"What do you mean 'chosen'?" Stryker asks, not letting it go. "You have to test for that kind of thing, do a screen test."

"I don't know, they waived it. Charlotte Belle requested you…what does it even matter," Jeremy says impatiently.

Stryker stops strumming his guitar. He never called Charlotte even though she gave him her number at the party months ago.

"I don't know Jeremy," Stryker says, resisting. "I'm not an actor."

"That's the thing, you are pretty much playing yourself. Just look pretty and smile at the camera." Jeremy can't understand why his client is being so difficult.

"Let me think about it," Stryker says.

"There's nothing to think about, it's a no-brainer. You don't have any new music coming out. I don't need you fading away into oblivion," Jeremy says angrily.

Stryker thinks for a second that maybe the publicity would get Luna's attention. Maybe it would remind her of how happy they were together.

"Ok—Ok, I'm in," Stryker agrees.

"Great, be on set next Thursday. I'll email you the details. See ya."

Stryker clicks off the call. He's anxious about seeing Charlotte Belle. After he ghosted her, Stryker wonders if she will give him an attitude.

Stryker is on set and the crew is milling about around him. It takes a lot of people to make a movie, Stryker thinks. No one on the sound stage is wearing masks, probably because several large contraptions are spouting antimicrobial chemical mist in each corner of the room. He approves of the clothes the stylist has given him, they're pretty much something he would wear in real life. Faded Levis and a white t-shirt. They have styled his blond hair to look like James Dean. It's cut short, brushed upward off his face, and in the very front is one big wave. Stryker's demeanor has changed since he lost Luna. He now has a brooding, tormented look, very much like the look James Dean was known for.

The makeup girl is fawning over him. Stryker looks incredibly sexy. His skin is smooth and doesn't require much makeup. Yet she's in his face, fussing over him with her full breasts almost touching his cheek.

"I think I'm good," he finally says. "You can stop now." Stryker's voice is deep, and he gives her the side eye.

The woman immediately stops what she's doing and rushes off. She can't wait to tell her friends she just made up Stryker Caine.

Stryker reads the section of the movie script he's to do. He's relieved he only has a few lines and hopes it will go by quickly. When he looks up from the script, he sees Charlotte Belle and Nikola Maltese approaching. Nikola ignores him while Charlotte walks right up to Stryker and greets him.

"Hi Stryker, so glad you could make it," Charlotte says with a wide smile.

She is in full makeup and Stryker is a little star struck. He has forgotten how beautiful she is. She has small pearl white baby teeth just like Julia Roberts. She's dressed as a cocktail waitress in a tight black satin corset and matching short shorts over black fishnet stockings. She's a knockout.

"Hi Charlotte," Stryker says, rising from his chair.

He feels awkward and doesn't know what else to say and hopes she will lead the conversation. Charlotte is 5'9" and even in her high heels Stryker towers over her. He can see Charlotte is checking him out, which makes him even more uncomfortable.

"This will be painless, I promise," she says, winking at him.

They are interrupted by the director, Chase Beckett's voice telling them they're ready to start. Chase introduces himself to Stryker. Charlotte, Nikola, and Stryker head over to where they will run the camera rehearsal. Chase tells Stryker where to stand and move. He explains they will go through the scene a few times so the camera crew can see what they're shooting.

The scene is set up as a low-lit dingy bar with several tables in front of the stage. Stryker is standing on stage with a back-up band—they are busy tuning and going over the set list. Charlotte plays a waitress and Nikola is a member of the audience.

Charlotte walks up to Nikola's table to take his order. Nikola suddenly grabs Charlotte's hand and pulls her across his lap as if to spank her. Charlotte struggles to get free. Stryker sees the commotion and calls out from the stage to Nikola.

"Hey! Let her go, that's not cool man!"

"Fuck you, mind your own fucking business," Nikola shouts back at him.

Nikola hold Charlotte's two wrists together so she can't

break free. Stryker jumps from the stage in front of the table. Nikola releases Charlotte's hands and as she scrambles to her feet he pushes her forward and she lands in Stryker's arms. With one swift move Stryker lets her go as Nikola stands up to confront him.

"You got a problem?" Nikola says.

The two men glare at each other, squaring off. They are approximately the same height and build.

"I said, have you got a problem?" Nikola says then puts his open palms on each side of Stryker's shoulders and shoves him backward with significant force.

"Hey, that's not in the script," Charlotte can be heard saying in the background.

Realizing Nikola has assaulted him for real, Stryker shoves Nikola so hard he knocks him off his feet. Nikola rises from the ground and Charlotte rushes between them.

"Cut!" Chase shouts.

"Nikola! That was so out of line," Charlotte yells.

"I was improvising," Nikolas mumbles, shooting Stryker a dirty look.

"Everyone get back in place. Let's run through it again for real and keep the shoving match," Chase says to them.

So much for being painless, Stryker thinks. After a few more takes, the actors get the scene and Chase announces it's a wrap.

"Well done everyone," Chase says, turning to the crew behind him.

Stryker sees the makeup girl behind Chase with her phone out taking pictures. He's tired and getting ready to leave when Charlotte stops him.

"Stryker, you did a great job, you're a natural," she says, placing her hand on his arm.

"Thanks."

"Come back to my trailer and we can celebrate your debut."

Stryker sees Charlotte's eyes are lit up with excitement and she has moved closer to him.

"Sorry, Charlotte. I'm late for rehearsal…we are in the studio working on new material."

I need to be anywhere but here, he thinks and walks away from her. Charlotte is miffed. She turns away and sees Nikola sitting in a chair moping. This has not gone anywhere near the way she planned.

It's the night of the 2025 ISMC Humanitarian Awards. Luna walks up to Simon's black self-driving limousine. She sees her reflection in the car's window as she opens the door. She's wearing another new designer evening gown. Now that Luna is an established influencer, famous designers clamor to send her extravagant gowns for her to wear to star filled events. For tonight's philanthropic event Luna chooses a rose pink strapless duchess satin gown by Aimon. The dress has a sweetheart neckline and fits close to her slender body. In her hand she carries a silver sequin clutch purse and wears heels with delicate crystal straps. She looks like royalty.

Simon is on a call, so he quietly acknowledges Luna as she settles into the back seat beside him. Her dress has a slit, and Luna has her legs crossed so her knee is exposed. She knows Simon will not touch her—she has set clear boundaries between them that Simon now respects. They have been working together for a month, and Luna is pleased how well she has cleaned up his presence on social media.

Luna is secretly impressed Simon is receiving a Humanitarian Award from the International Society of Medical Crusaders. ISMC is known globally for providing medical aid and protecting mankind. For that universally respected medical organization to have chosen Simon Caswell must mean he does have some redeeming qualities, Luna thinks.

Cautiously she observes Simon while he's on his phone. *Has she gotten him all wrong? Is his obnoxious behavior just a cover? Is he truly a compassionate human being aiding those less fortunate?*

Luna occupies herself by scrolling through her *Flikrz* feed. She stops scrolling when she sees @Celebweekly has posted a photo of Stryker with the actress Charlotte Belle on the set of her new movie. Stryker is holding Charlotte in his arms—she is wearing a black bustier and black hot pants. The caption reads: *Stryker Caine in an upcoming film with Charlotte Belle. For more on this duo that no one saw coming see link in our bio.*

Luna does not read any further and slips her phone into her fancy purse. Simon clicks off his call and smiles at her.

"Good evening gorgeous," he says.

"Hello, Simon."

Simon is in a black tuxedo and Luna hates to admit it, but he does look handsome.

"Are you ready with your speech?" she asks.

This is a big moment for him, and she doesn't want Simon to screw it up by going off script.

"I'm always ready, Luna. I predicted I would win this award months ago." Simon smirks arrogantly.

When they arrive at the venue, they are greeted with the fanfare of photographers on the red carpet. To gloat over winning his award Simon stops to talk to every reporter he can. Luna tries to make herself invisible and walks inside the auditorium to take her seat.

This is one of the biggest events of the year with many famous dignitaries from all over the world. The virus testing requires a blood sample from each attendee. Luna puts her hand palm up through a gray tube at the entryway. Her finger is pricked for a blood sample.

She sees multiple senators, other politicians, and people from the entertainment industry. There are even people from the United Nations. Luna couldn't have asked for anything more to improve Simon's image.

As the lights go down and the orchestra begins playing, Simon makes his way to sit beside her. Luna feels important being at this event and with the man of honor, Simon Caswell. She wonders if maybe she does like this environment and perhaps she should give Simon a chance. *It's clear Stryker has moved on and is busy dating movie stars. Why shouldn't I be happy too?*

The announcer steps up to the podium and begins speaking. "This year's ISMC Humanitarian Award recognizes the work of Simon Caswell. We are forever grateful he has devoted himself to the welfare of humanity in communities throughout the United States and internationally!"

There's thunderous applause as Simon makes his way between the seats to the stage. Once the audience stops clapping, Luna listens intently to his speech.

"Thank you. Thank you, this award means a lot to me. I believe in eliminating the suffering and pain of others. With each waking breath I take, I become even more committed to aiding those less fortunate…"

Simon goes on speaking for a good ten minutes. His speech is riveting. He speaks about the starving children in Africa and how he has held brown babies in his arms and fed them. He talks about helping families in America destroyed by COVID-25 by personally providing them with food and water.

When Simon finishes speaking the audience rises to their feet and claps almost endlessly until Simon leaves the stage. Luna is moved close to tears. She desperately wants to congratulate him and apologize for treating him so coldly all this time.

She hurries backstage and finds Simon in the hallway outside the green room. He has his back turned and is engrossed in a conversation with Penelope, clutching his award and laughing cheerfully. Luna stops in her tracks so as not to interrupt them. She knows filming Simon at this moment will be golden for use on his social media sites, so she takes out her phone, places her clutch under her forearm, and begins recording.

"So Penelope, how did I do?" he asks.

"You were marvelous Simon, so believable. Half the audience was crying," Penelope says.

"I pieced together my speech with excerpts from TED Talks on poverty off the internet." Simon laughs.

"I will Venmo the final payment to ISMC from an 'unknown source' as soon as I can," Penelope says.

"Good. It proves everyone can be bought, Penelope. Even ISMC…and of course Luna."

"If she ever finds out you really could care less about repairing your image, that it's just a ploy to get her into bed…" Penelope snickers.

"Just remember, don't leave an electronic trail," Simon warns.

"Right, this is the last thing we want on social." Penelope chuckles.

"It's too late," Luna says. "I'm uploading it to *Flikrz* now."

Simon whirls around to face Luna, his face pale white with fear. Penelope is covering her mouth with both hands.

"What?" Simon says, stepping toward her.

"Don't come near me, Simon," Luna shouts.

"Did you really do it? It's on *Flikrz*?" Simon takes a step toward her.

Terrified Simon might tackle her and wrestle the phone away, her hands shake, but she's able to hit the button to upload it.

"It's on the Cloud now for safekeeping," Luna says.

"So, it's not on *Flikrz*?" Penelope asks, frightened.

"It can be anytime I choose. For right now it's on my iCloud."

"How much do you want, Luna?" Simon asks.

He puts his award down by his feet and takes out his phone. "I can Venmo you as much as you want right now."

"You are such a lowlife, Simon…" She feels like spitting on him. "I don't want your money. I don't want anything from you."

"Everyone wants something…" Penelope says.

"Be quiet Penelope, just shut your mouth." Simon growls.

For a moment, the three stand motionless, not speaking, until Luna says calmly, "There is something I need."

"Name it," Simon replies.

"I want out of my contract with you. You are a piece of garbage," Luna says, emboldened.

"You got it. You have my word. Just don't release the video. Do you promise?" Simon replies in a condescending tone.

"Your word is worthless." Luna seethes.

Simon turns to Penelope. "Have my lawyer write something up breaking the contract ASAP."

"Yes Simon, immediately," Penelope replies, running down the hall.

"See Luna, it will be done," Simon says, attempting to smile at her.

Luna rolls her eyes. "I never want to see you again," she says and walks down the hallway away from Simon Caswell for what she hopes will be forever.

CHAPTER 11

RYDER MADDOX, A top influencer, and his entourage approach the glass dome where Coachella 2025 is being held. This is the first time the Coachella festival has happened since the virus began in 2019. The valley is completely enclosed on all sides, radiating down from the top of the dome are rainbow colored glass panels. The festival's dome is 400 feet high and stretches for miles across a lush green valley. Encircling the dome are huge mechanical units with giant hoses connected to holes in the glass structure. Each hole is large enough for people to enter through. Security teams dressed in all black stand outside each of the hose's entryways.

Luna is excited to be included in Ryder's crew. She embraces the festival culture and is wearing a multi-colored string bikini top that barely contains her ample D-cup breasts—her tight brown suede short shorts blend with her brown skin giving the appearance she is bottomless. On her feet are fire-engine red patent leather platform boots. Her long black curly hair is loose and wild. Around her neck are several beaded necklaces, and numerous beaded bracelets are on both wrists. Luna looks fierce and she feels like a superhero.

Along with Ryder and Luna there are four people in Ryder's group, all of them are wearing fashionable masks. Samantha, an influencer from New England, a Hollywood stylist named Micaela, Kate, a make-up artist, and Brad. No one knows what Brad's occupation is other than to constantly hang around Ryder. Each of them is eager to begin their adventure. Not only does the group have tickets to get inside the festival venue, they also are invited to Coachella's 2025 *Outstanding in The Field*—a lavish four-course family style meal served on a long wooden table in the VIP Rose Garden.

At each of the hose's entrances hundreds of people assemble in single file to gain entry to the event. As VIPs Ryder, Luna, and the rest of the group bypass the line and walk to the RDVT machines. Ryder steps up and swipes the app on his phone over the kiosk. Once he's identified he inserts his forearm into the Rapid DNA Viral Testing tube. A green light flashes while a computer generated voice declares him virus free. Samantha goes next and gets the green light approval. Micaela, Luna, and Kate subsequently follow, and all are approved. Brad is the last to be tested, and Luna notices his face is shiny with sweat as he puts his forearm into the testing cylinder. A red light goes off and the automated voice announces, "Virus detected, virus detected. Failed!"

"Oh, like really Brad?" Ryder says, scolding him.

"You are such a fuck-up. Come along with me ladies, into the dome we go."

With that Ryder and the women abandon Brad and walk through the hose pipeline into the festival. Right before she steps inside Luna turns to look over her shoulder and sees Brad looking forlorn as security staff approach him from all sides.

Luna steps out of the hose into Coachella and is instantly swept up into a mystical experience. Music is playing everywhere, different genres and sounds colliding. Bands are continually changing on the rotating stages elevated above the crowd on hydraulic platforms. Hundreds of concert goers are on the grass occupied in various forms of activity. People are getting food at the bevy of food trucks parked in a circle. Others are climbing on monumental sculptures or are balancing themselves in assorted Yoga poses on the festival grounds. Popup Art studios displaying artistry are in blue tents, and a 200-foot-high white Ferris wheel revolves in the distance.

"Holy shit!" Ryder exclaims. "We are in Utopia."

Stryker is in a self-driving volocopter, heading to Coachella. He's a last-minute replacement on the performance line-up. The pop group Planet X canceled as their lead singer was suddenly struck ill with COVID-25. There wasn't time to organize the entire band, so Stryker is playing an acoustic solo.

The volocopter lands in a field, and Stryker is tested for COVID-25. He's virus free and enters the Coachella dome. The atmosphere reminds him of Burning Man but not as intense. He sees a crush of humanity, music, and art. He's to perform on Stage 5, and he makes his way in that direction, sidestepping several float handlers maneuvering a long chain of enormous helium balloons hundreds of feet above the concertgoers. Stryker is pleased there's so much chaos around him he can go about his way unnoticed.

⁂

Luna is the center of attention, sitting in the middle of the long dinner table at the *Outstanding in The Field* feast. She purposely chose the seat so she could mingle with as many guests as possible. Everyone at the table is either famous or knows someone famous. Luna is both. She now travels in circles of superstars and their companions and is completely at ease. She can't even remember the days when she was a meek recluse living in a tiny apartment in New York City.

There are huge television screens mounted on stands around the table displaying the musical acts from the concert. Each screen is dedicated to one of the six stages.

"Does anyone know where we are in the lineup," Ryder asks no one in particular.

"Drake was today's headliner. Then it was Taylor Swift…so next up is The Weeknd, Planet X, and Bad Bunny…" a thirty-something man says.

He's wearing clever wire rimmed glasses, sitting across from Luna, and staring at her chest.

"When is Lady Gaga?" a woman asks.

"She's tomorrow on Stage 5," Luna answers.

For the second course the servers bring large bowls heaping with organic sweet corn succotash, a platter of tuna empanadas, and trays of melon slices wrapped in prosciutto.

The food is placed on the table and the man is disappointed all the dishware is partially blocking his view of Luna.

"Oh, this all looks so good," she says, her eyes lighting up.

"It does. It does," the man says, smiling, catching glimpses of Luna's cleavage as she serves herself.

&

Stryker is ready to go on stage and waits for the emcee to break it to the crowd he will be replacing the extremely popular group, Planet X.

"People…are you enjoying yourselves?" the emcee shouts into the microphone.

The thousands of concert goers cheer.

"I said, are you enjoying yourselves?" The emcee shouts even louder.

The crowd responds with more cheering.

"Good!… Good…due to circumstances beyond their control Planet X regretfully had to cancel at the last minute…"

The crowd boos loudly in disappointment. Stryker is jittery, wondering if they will continue to boo when he walks on stage.

"Wait, Wait! We are lucky to have an amazing performer you all know…" The emcee motions to Stryker to come up the steps onto the platform.

"…I present to you Stryker Caine!"

The crowd goes wild. Stryker is relieved and waves his arms in greeting. He approaches the microphone stand and speaks. "Thank you, thank you. It's an honor to be here with you, to be a part of the most amazing festival in the world."

He plucks a string on his guitar and shakes his blond hair out of his eyes. The concert goers whistle and scream his name. Stryker feeds off the energy from the crowd and launches into his first song.

"By the way, I'm Max," the man in the glasses says to Luna.

Luna looks at Max. *Well he's not famous, so he must be here with someone who is.* Max is looking back at Luna, hoping to develop a connection with her. He has dark hair, brown eyes, and a lanky build. Luna studies him. *Not really my type at all.* She knows she's been alone too long as Santana often reminds her. *Maybe I should totally not shoot him down.* She says, "I'm Luna. What do you do? Who are you here with?"

Max is a little taken aback to be put on the spot this way. *Geez, I guess I need to qualify to get her attention.*

"I'm here with the film crew. I'm a producer."

"There hasn't been much produced in Hollywood these days with all the corona out there." Luna realizes after she says it, not only is she shooting him down, she's being downright rude. I am so out of practice, she thinks and tries to soften her words. "But you never know, there are ways around it."

"Exactly, most of my work is done with computer generated actors."

Luna is surprised by his answer and is now interested

in what this man has to say. "Really? That's fascinating..." Luna says, tilting her head toward him.

"Indeed, the possibilities are endless." Max smiles.

Maybe I do have a chance with her, he thinks.

❧

Stryker has played two songs and announces to the crowd, "Here is a song I wrote during a very dark period in my life. It's about love found and love lost."

Stryker sings the first verse of his hit song, "Luna."

"Luna where did you go?

You shut me down and blocked the road

We were on a whirl wind high; you know I felt so justified..."

Dessert is being served when a woman sitting beside Ryder looks up at the huge television screen across from her.

"That's not Planet X...who is that? I love that song!" the woman says to Ryder.

"That's Stryker Caine. Heeey Luna, he's playing your song." Ryder leans forward to look at Luna.

Luna's face is aghast when she looks at the television monitor. *Oh my God! It's Stryker.* She hasn't seen him since she broke up with him in New York and feels a rush of anxiety setting in.

"Stryker Caine? I love his music, what is this song called again?" Max asks innocently. "Oh right, it's called Luna... how coincidental," Max says, smiling at Luna.

Everyone at the table turns to look at Luna. She's motionless as she stares at the television screen, tears welling up in her eyes.

Ryder looks at Max and puts his index finger to his lips, hushing him. He mouths the words, "That's Luna's ex."

Max looks at Luna and sees she's getting emotional. He can see she still must be hung up on this guy and knows he's lost any opportunity to get to know her better.

Luna blinks rapidly, holding back her tears. *He will not ruin this day for me. He is nothing to me, that was a lifetime ago!*

"That was a delicious meal," Samantha says, trying to clear the air.

"It certainly was," Luna says, thankful Samantha has changed the subject.

"It was delicious. We should make our way back to the concert," Ryder says, putting his cloth napkin on his plate and standing up.

Who cares if I see Stryker on stage? Luna rises from her chair. *I look hot and can't wait until he sees me. He'll see what he lost.*

Stryker is nearly finished with his set. Every time he plays the song "Luna," it feels a little cathartic. Today's no different. Stryker smiles throughout the whole song. His mind drifts back to when he was with Luna. The way she wrinkled up her brown nose when she smelled something bad. Her contagious laugh. To him it now seems ages ago when he held her in his arms and remembers how he loved her so much. Stryker ends the song but doesn't want to leave the crowd with such a melancholy tune.

"Here we go!" he growls into the microphone, and

he begins playing energetically his first hit song "Quarantina." The crowd goes crazy and sings in unison the chorus, "Quarantina, Quarantina!" Stryker shakes back his blond hair—his mind and body immersed in the song as he feeds off the crowd's enthusiasm.

Ryder and his crew slowly make their way through the crowd, headed in no particular direction. Luna hears the music and the familiar song. She flashes back to the time when Stryker played it at the Fury then grabbed her in the hallway and kissed her so intensely.

"This way!" She gets ahead of Ryder and beckons them all to follow her. She picks up the pace, wanting to get to Stage 5 and see Stryker. Or actually she wants Stryker to see her. Ryder is bothered that Luna has taken control of his entourage, but he follows behind her, nonetheless. He's surprised how determined she is, pushing people aside as she squeezes through their shoulders. *She is on a mission!*

By the time the group arrives at Stage 5, the music has stopped and the crowd is hollering and applauding. Luna is out of breath, her chest heaving, as she watches Stryker climb down from the stage and disappear into the massive crowd.

CHAPTER 12

STRYKER FEELS BEST when surfing. He's not confined to the limitations of the Pandemic—he is free and his mind is clear.

Logan is with him. It's dusk and the two men have been surfing most of the day except for breaks to drink beer from their cooler. The beach is private, and Stryker is finally enjoying himself. He's not thinking about Luna, Charlotte, or any woman. He is a free agent.

They load their surfboards into the Jeep at around 8:00 p.m. Stryker has consumed a lot of beer, so he lets Logan drive. The roads are dangerously narrow and wind tightly around the hills on the Southern California coast. Without warning Logan turns off the main road and drives down a dirt pathway onto the beach.

"You want to catch some more waves Logan?" Stryker asks.

"No. There's an amazing party up here, and I want to avoid the paparazzi. We can go in the back way," Logan says, parking the Jeep on the sand.

It's a beautiful night on the beach, and the repetition of

the waves hitting the shore is hypnotic. There's a long trail of stone steps leading up to a massive house on a steep hill. Looking up at the house on the top of the steps, Stryker sees lights in the windows, hears the clanking of dishware and people talking and laughing. Together, Logan and Stryker start climbing upward. Halfway up the steps they pass an infinity swimming pool. Stryker glances at the sparkling water on the pool's surface. It shines in the moonlight and looks so inviting.

When they reach the stone patio outside the house, they try to blend into the crowd and look inconspicuous. Several small drones carrying trays of cocktails coast amongst the guests. Stryker and Logan grab drinks off a drink drone hovering beside them and then slip underneath a tree in the corner.

"Isn't this the life, Stryker? I never thought I would live this way," Logan says.

Stryker looks around the stone patio where people stand in small groups. They all seem to be having a good time, carefree, at ease in their posh surroundings. There's an abundance of plush seating to choose from. Giant pillows fill the white furniture and there are several mini gazebos with white curtains. In the center of the veranda is a large fountain spouting water, filling the shelves of bowls beneath it.

"Wow, I spot a beauty over there," Logan says, watching a young woman across the courtyard. A classic California girl with long blonde hair and sun kissed skin, she's looking in their direction, and Logan hopes she's looking at him and not Stryker, which is so often the case. Stryker usually gets all the attention whenever they go out together.

"Go for it man," Stryker says, plopping down on a chair, the soft pillows enveloping his body. "I'm going to have another drink."

Logan walks off. Stryker is pleased to see his friend so happy and puts his hand up, indicating to a drone to bring him another drink. The drink drone flies over, and Stryker scoops up two drinks off the platter. He settles into his chair situated in the shadows away from everyone. He knows he has the perfect seat to people watch.

After a while he gets bored watching the vapid, self-absorbed party-goers. He decides to go back down the stone steps he came up to find some solitude. By now, he has had a lot to drink and must steady himself so as not to tumble down the steps. He regains his balance and sees the roaring ocean waves behind the edge of the infinity pool. It appears as if the pool's still water just drops off into the sea. He steps onto the pool's deck. It's a warm sticky night, and Stryker's shirt is wet with sweat and clinging to his muscular body. Doubting any of the guests will venture down such a treacherous foot trail, he peels off his shirt, kicks off his sandals, and strips down until he's completely naked. With outstretched arms, he dives into the undisturbed water.

Chapter 13

SANTANA IS DRIVING Luna's red 2025 Porsche Boxster convertible with Luna in the passenger's seat. He has been talking nonstop all week about Cosmo Octavius, his favorite social media star, who has been posting on social continuously about his party in Malibu and all the different celebrities that will be there. Santana is enamored with Cosmo Octavius and really wants to meet him. Finding out the location of the party and getting an invitation was nearly impossible, but Luna would do anything for Santana, so she contacted her influencer associates to get the inside scoop of where the party would be located.

The party is right on the beach on a hilltop. Luna has already done the celebrity party scene and is not fazed by the names of the people supposedly attending. She's more than willing to go out that evening though as Santana is a lively companion and always makes her laugh. He's wearing a turquoise blue shirt, white dress shorts with summer loafers. He looks like a celebrity, Luna thinks, he will blend right in.

Santana is excited about the party and can't erase his big grin. The sides of his head are shaved, and the rest of his black hair is pulled to the back of his head in a man bun. Santana is from Ecuador and sings along to a song in Spanish playing on the car's stereo. His index fingers tap the steering wheel to the beat. When Stryker's hit song "Luna" comes on the radio next, he quickly turns to another station.

"Luna, is Ryder Maddox going to be there?" Santana asks.

"He was invited. We'll see if he shows up," Luna replies.

Luna is wearing a romantic white summer dress. It's short with a delicate eyelet design. The thin white straps keep falling down onto her bare shoulders. The lightweight fabric pierced with small holes is laid out in a flowerlike pattern. Her brown skin is peeking through the textile and the top of her breasts are on display. Luna knows she looks hot.

They pull into the circular driveway, and Santana hands the car keys to the valet. Luna and Santana make their way through the shouting paparazzi and duck inside the immense dwelling. In the foyer they are promptly tested for COVID-25 by a rapid testing machine that takes a tiny droplet of their blood. They are then sprayed with the customary antimicrobial chemical mist and find their way out onto the luxurious patio that runs along the entire side of the mansion overlooking the ocean. It's made of flagstone with a giant fountain in the center.

Luna hopes tonight she will meet non celebrities like Santana—people whose lives don't revolve around social media celebrity gossip. She knows most of the people at the party are there only to promote themselves, yet Luna has faith she will meet someone who is down to earth.

Luna and Santana grab themselves summer cocktails

off a drink drone and mingle with the guests. The people they meet are exceedingly wealthy. They speak in monotone voices about themselves in the third person. Santana is in his element, thrilled to be around such affluent people. He's talking with his hands, making grand gestures. Luna stands quietly beside him and smiles every so often, pretending to be engaged.

At this point in her life Luna feels good about herself. She has changed so much and has come into her own. Plus, she feels empowered after the incident with Simon Caswell. She is no longer a victim. She turned the tables on a powerful man and won.

After some time passes, Luna finds it tiresome to continue listening to people brag about how successful they are. Santana is so wrapped up talking he barely notices when she excuses herself and leaves the group of celebrities to walk along the perimeter of the patio, trying to avoid getting swept into another circle of guests' conversations. She wants to get away from the beautiful people and get closer to the ocean. Leaning on the patio's railing, she breathes in the refreshing salt air. From there she sees stone steps leading to the beach and halfway down is an infinity swimming pool. I can go put my toes in the water, she thinks. It's so hot out.

Luna begins descending and is glad she wore flat sandals so she can maneuver herself safely over the wobbly stone steps. Once at the pool deck, she removes her sandals and walks up to the edge of the pool. She hears the lapping of water and realizes someone is swimming. A head bobs up and down, coming toward her. Suddenly the person rises from the water with such force the water splatters her feet.

Luna takes two steps backward and gasps. It's Stryker! When he sees her, he shakes his head and brushes back his wet hair with both hands, blinking water from his eyes.

It's Luna, her white dress puffing up from the cool breeze off the ocean. *Am I hallucinating? Can this be real?*

"Luna?" he says.

Her heart melts. She hasn't seen Stryker since she slammed the door in his face in New York City over a year ago. He smiles, resting his forearms on the side of the pool. His muscular chest glistens wet, his hair slicked back. Luna feels the same rush of awe she felt when they first met on the roof. He took her breath away, he was so handsome.

Stryker can't believe he's finally found Luna. He had given up all hope. Now here she is, a vision in white looking like an angel in the moonlight.

"What are you doing here?" Stryker stammers.

Luna feels sweat trickling down her ribs from her armpits but knows she has to hold it together. The oceans' waves rumble loudly beyond the edge of the pool. To avoid eye contact with Stryker she looks to the left, watching the waves crashing onto the beach.

"I came down here to cool off," she says. "Not that it's any of your business."

To get away from him, Luna walks to the opposite end of the pool. "Don't take this as an invitation to talk to me... like I said, I just came down to cool off."

After a moment Luna walks down the pools immense steps into the shallow water up to her calves. Stryker floats in the center of the pool, and Luna realizes he's naked. She's surprised how at peace she feels. The sky is full of stars and the moonlight is reflecting on the water. Luna quickly shakes herself out of feeling the romantic atmosphere. She had hoped at this point she would never see Stryker again. Now that Europe is starting to let Americans travel into their borders, Luna assumed he would have moved overseas.

Stryker remains in the deep end, swimming from one side of the pool to the other. He only has one opportunity to explain to Luna he still has deep feelings for her and see if she still has feelings for him. He knows he must choose his words carefully. He looks at her so far away from him in the pool and speaks from his heart.

"Luna, I realize it seems like I intentionally tried to hurt you..."

"What? I really don't want to hear it...you slept with some supermodel hours after we broke up."

"I never slept with that woman. It was a set-up from the start. I was so drunk I could barely walk, and she took advantage of that. I must have passed out in her apartment. I was knocked out cold when she took that photo of us. All she wanted was more attention on social media." Stryker stops there for a moment, collecting his thoughts.

"So, you didn't sleep with her?" Luna questions.

"No. I didn't. I'm sorry, you are the only woman I wanted to be with. I know now I should have been straight with you."

Stryker slowly moves toward her in the pool. Luna has her arms crossed over her chest. She refuses to look at him and is looking away at the ocean in the distance so doesn't notice he's swimming closer to her.

"Luna, you are the only woman I ever felt a connection

with. I realize what I had with you was a once in a lifetime love. I would do anything to get you back and show you the person I have become."

Luna is thinking back to that summer day when he first introduced himself to her from his fire escape. She questioned his name then, and he had said earnestly that it was Stryker, Stryker Caine.

"You lied to me outright, even about your real name."

"My middle name is Stryker. I had to use my middle name to get a fresh start in the music business. I understand what I did was terribly wrong…in the past I thought I was entitled to whatever I wanted because of who my family was… I am a different person now. I have grown so much since then. I know now if I wanted you to be part of my life, I should have told you who I really was," Stryker pleads.

Not convinced, Luna responds with pride. "I have grown too. I was naïve. I am much more discerning now and have a lot more experience dealing with people who lie. I am not the trustworthy person you met…"

Stryker interrupts her. "I understand and respect the fact you have gained much more experience. You never needed me to become successful, and I always believed you could do it on your own."

Luna likes hearing him acknowledge how well she's doing in her career. The fact that he recognizes she's a star in her industry. She feels her mood soften…but not entirely. Stryker sees from her body language he's slowly disarming her, so he continues. "But being without the one you love is not being successful at all. Is it?"

Luna is quiet, considering what Stryker says. It's

true she is hugely successful and wealthy. Yet she feels an immense void in her life without him.

"After everything that happened…making it as a musician and the world finding out who my father is. Being rich and famous, I realize, doesn't mean you can get whatever you want. I wanted so much to get you back," Stryker grovels.

Still looking toward the ocean, Luna says in a low vulnerable voice, "Well, how hard did you even try."

Stryker slowly approaches. Perhaps he's breaking down her defenses.

"I can't really hear you." Stryker says as he seizes the moment and suddenly disappears beneath the water. Coming to the surface he's relieved to see Luna is still standing there and has not run off. Their eyes meet, and he can see by the softening of her gaze she still has feelings for him.

She still has her arms folded across her body when Stryker reaches around her and gently pulls her into the pool. Luna is startled. She didn't expect Stryker to touch her, much less pull her into the pool. She falls forward against his body as the water washes around them. Stryker doesn't let her go.

Luna floats in his arms with her hands on his shoulders. She can't help but stare into his sky-blue eyes, their noses almost touching.

Stryker is overwhelmed, feeling Luna so close to him. Their lips meet as if for the first time, her dress floating up around her on the surface. Stryker feels her naked body—her nipples, her waist. Putting his hands on each of her cheeks he pulls her to him. She can feel his arousal firmly against her and caught up in the moment relaxes her body.

"Now my dress is all wet," Luna whispers.

Stryker swiftly unravels her dress from behind, and in one sweeping movement he pulls it up over her head and tosses it on the pool deck.

Logan has struck out trying to flirt with the blonde woman on the patio. She has walked off and left him standing awkwardly alone with a drink in his hand. He looks back to where Stryker was sitting. Seeing the white plush chairs are empty, he scans the patio but doesn't see any sign of Stryker. He walks to the edge of the patio to look at the ocean. When he looks down, he sees two people in the swimming pool, a woman standing in the shallow end…and a man treading water in the deep end. He realizes it's Stryker and Luna, and it doesn't appear to be going well for Stryker.

Two of the guests, a man and a woman, join him.

"What a beautiful night. So many stars," the man exclaims to anyone in earshot.

"Look. Look, there's someone in the pool," the woman says, pointing over the railing. "Isn't that Stryker Caine?"

"Who is he with?" the man says, leaning forward.

"I think that's Luna James," the woman cries out.

A few more people come to the railing to look, and one of them says, "Weren't they a couple way back when?"

"Right, he wrote that hit song about her."

Oh no, I've got to do something, so he doesn't mess this up, Logan thinks, rushing away.

A growing crowd of guests form on the edge of the patio. The influencers whip out their phones, knowing this is a golden opportunity to take advantage and post *Stryker and Luna back together again?* on their social media feeds.

Luna and Stryker hear someone rustling up the stone steps. A figure comes to the top of the landing, and as he steps forward Luna and Stryker are surprised see it's Logan.

"Thank God you've found each other. Do you know what a mess this guy has been?" Logan says, trying to catch his breath.

The last thing Logan saw was Luna at the end of the pool with her arms crossed. Now Logan rushes to the side of the pool, quickly gathering up Luna's wet dress and Stryker's shorts and t-shirt. He scurries back down the steps, shouting over his shoulder as he descends, "Now the two of you will have to talk and work it out!"

"Dude, are you crazy?" Stryker yells at him as Logan runs away with their clothing.

"I'm not crazy, you better work it out, I can't have you make the second biggest mistake of your life," Logan calls out as he disappears out of view.

Both Luna and Stryker look up to the house above the pool and see the crowd of guests pointing and filming them. Apparently, they have become the main attraction of the party. Stryker and Luna turn to each other.

"How are we going to get out of the pool without being filmed by all these people?" Luna says.

"Why do we need to get out of the pool. Let's just make the best of it," Stryker says, pulling her back into his arms.

Just when you thought it was over
THE LUNA JAMES TRILOGY
continues with the next book

STRYKER STRIKES BACK

Learn more at elenagreyrock.com

Songs by Arturo Augustus

Convertible

Feeling so alive on a sun-drenched day
Wind swept hair all around her face

Her laughter seems to come from every side
Fills up the air and takes me for a ride

Time was never better with the top pulled down
We make our way through gas filled towns

Full throttle speed another pitstop
Wheels spinning up to a coffee shop

Fading from ourselves and chasing down the sun
No better time to be on the run

Time was never better with the top pulled down
We make our way through gas filled towns

The glow of sunshine never leaves her face
with a radiant smile in its full embrace

Day turns to night on a frenzy ride
Dust covered roads and moon lit lines

Time was never better with the top pulled down
We make our way through gas filled towns

Quarantina

Did you fall down did you hit the ground or did you
make your way around
quarantina quarantina

were you paralyzed were you hypnotized were you
petrified by
quarantina quarantina

Did you scream and shout did you thrash about and
wonder how you got to
quarantina quarantina

When humankind fell far behind this frightful time were
you blinded by
quarantina quarantina

And if you made it through would it occur to you your
life is now just a
quarantina quarantina

So take the time to look around
And finally crawl out from your underground

Just another quarantina quarantina

quarantina quarantina, quarantina quarantina

Luna

Luna, where did you go,
Shut me down and blocked the road

3000 miles and no headlights
Broken down and full of fight

All of me just for you, it's all I ever really knew
But All of me you'll ever see is liiies

We were on a whirlwind high, you know I felt so justified
Should have given you every part—even if it meant
my heart

All of me just for you, it's all I ever really knew
But All of me you'll ever see is liiies

You left me badly ripped and torn
beaten down and oh so worn

Walking down these lonely tracks
felt the cold wind on my back

All of me just for you, it's all I ever really knew

I hear the train the whistle blows it asks me where I want
to go
One last stop, one more try but you won't be waiting on
the other side

If I find my way back to you—I'll show the world they never knew

All of me just for you, you know it's all I could ever do
All of me just for you, it's all I ever wanted to

Quarantini Recipe

Green Intensity Quarantini

Ingredients
2.5 oz Absolut Elyx vodka
.5 oz simple syrup
.5 oz lime juice
4 basil leaves
1 slice jalapeño

Instructions
Place all ingredients into a shaker, then shake and strain into a freshly chilled martini glass. Garnish with another thin slice of jalapeño.

More Quarantini recipes